He leaned over and adjusted something on the saddle of Mrs. Pollifax's horse, except that whatever adjustment he made did not appear to please her horse. It snorted, reared in alarm and took off—there was no other word for it; her horse took off like a jet plane in ascension—so fast there was neither time for Mrs. Pollifax to breathe or to scream, the problem of survival being immediate and consuming as she struggled to stay mounted on ths huge creature gone mad.

Down the length of the meadow they flew, she and the horse joined together by only the most fleeting of contact: Mrs. Pollifax hanging on in desperation.

"The United States' most senior—and most eccentric—operative. Told with the incomparable wit and charm for which Dorothy Gilman and her heroine are justifiably famous. *Mrs. Pollifax on the China Station* will attract a host of fans, old and new, to match the success of her previous bestsellers."

Mystery News

MRS. POLLIFAX ON THE CHINA STATION

Dorothy Gilman

FAWCETT CREST • NEW YORK

A Fawcett Crest Book
Published by Ballantine Books
Copyright © 1983 by Dorothy Gilman Butters

Library of Congress Catalog Card Number: 82-45972

ISBN 0-449-20417-0

This edition published by arrangement with Doubleday & Company, Inc.

Manufactured in the United States of America

First Ballantine Books Edition: October 1984

With special thanks to David Ownby, China guide,
for sharing his knowledge of the country, and
for his translations and advice.

MRS. POLLIFAX SAT IN CARSTAIRS' OFFICE WITH A CUP OF coffee in one hand and a sandwich in the other, her hat an inverted bowl of blue felt with such a cockeyed twist to its brim that Bishop guessed it had been frequently sat on and squashed. He saw her glance at Carstairs, seated behind his desk, and then at him, and now she said gently, "Yes, the weather's been unseasonably cool for May, and my trip to Langley Field very pleasant, we've discussed my geraniums and how I met Cyrus Reed in Zambia, but I really do think—"

Bishop put down his own coffee cup and grinned. He thought this must be how she appeared to her garden clubs—a cheerful, cozy little woman with fly-away white hair and a penchant for odd hats and growing geraniums—

and he thought it a pity he couldn't share with those garden clubs his first meeting with her in this office, just after she'd led an escape party out of Albania against incredible odds, and had been whisked back to this country by jet. She had sat in this same chair, wearing the voluminous clothes of a goat-herder's wife, her face as dark as a gypsy's after three days adrift in the Adriatic, and what she'd accomplished had staggered them all. He sometimes felt it was impossible to reconcile these two Emily Pollifaxes; his grin deepened as he said, "You're suggesting we dispense with pleasantries and get on with it?"

"Well," she pointed out, "it's difficult to believe you've brought me here to discuss the weather. *Really* difficult," she added with a twinkle, "considering that you sent a private plane for me, which I must say was dashing of you."

"We do try to be dashing when we can," Bishop told her gravely. "It counteracts the soiled trench-coat image that—" He stopped, remembering Mrs. Pollifax's reproachful telephone calls to him when a scandal about the CIA surfaced. *But that wasn't our department,* he would tell her, and point out that he really couldn't relay her indignation to the White House. He supposed that it was this quality in her that led Carstairs to brief her more carefully than he did his other agents, but her responses were never more surprising to Bishop than the fruit cakes she sent at Christmas, which usually incapacitated the entire department, their brandy fumes lingering almost as long as the hangovers.

Suddenly he remembered why Mrs. Pollifax was here, and what Carstairs was going to propose to her, and he felt that old clutch of horror that always hit him when she sat innocently on the edge of her chair, all eagerness and delight at a new assignment, and always chiding him for his concern. It was rather like an attack of violent indigestion, and he wondered if Carstairs was feeling it too; if so, he gave no evidence of it. Not yet at least. He would eventually, of course; he always did.

"The job we have in mind," Carstairs began smoothly, "is innocuous enough on the surface, Mrs. Pollifax, but because of the country involved could be extremely dangerous—extremely—if you came under suspicion." He gazed at her thoughtfully. "Which is why I wanted you here personally, to make sure you understand this, and to ask whether you still feel—are still interested—"

"What country?" she promptly asked.

"The People's Republic of China."

She drew in her breath sharply. "But how incredibly exciting," she breathed, "and what an amazing coincidence! I've been so curious, so interested—"

"*Extremely* dangerous," Bishop heard himself say firmly.

Her eyes widened. "But you say that about all the assignments," she told him, "and surely we're friends with China now?"

"Exactly," Carstairs said lightly, "which makes it all the more shocking if any suspicions should be aroused. But we have some business there that simply can't be handled through diplomatic channels, and we've decided to chance it."

"Chance what?" asked Mrs. Pollifax cheerfully.

"Roughly speaking," he said, "we want to get a man *out* of China, but to do this we must first get a man *into* China—an agent, of course—to accomplish this. Your job, if you take this on, would be to provide cover for this agent, and at a certain point approach a certain native—*not* an agent—who's known to have some helpful information."

Mrs. Pollifax said warmly, "Well, that sounds easy enough to—"

Bishop interrupted her. "Of course it sounds easy and innocuous," he said indignantly, "because he hasn't mentioned that in making this contact in Xian you become

absolutely expendable—all to guard the identity of someone else—and that this man in Xian, who is *not* an agent,
could just as easily turn you over to the People's Security
Bureau, for all we know about him.''

Carstairs looked at him incredulously; in an icy voice he
said, ''My dear Bishop, all our people become expendable
when they take on a job, you know that and so does Mrs.
Pollifax. I've already told her it's dangerous.'' He turned
back to her and said stiffly, ''Bishop is right, of course,
and you *would* be risking exposure at that point, but to this
I would add that it's of value to us that you do not speak
Chinese, and would not speak it either in your sleep or
under drugs; that you've endured interrogations before,
and have shown a remarkable ability to sustain the role of
Aggrieved and Misunderstood Tourist. I have every hope
that such talents wouldn't be needed, of course, but still—
despite Bishop's inexplicable attack of sentiment,'' he said,
giving him a quelling glance, ''he is perfectly right.''

''Sorry, sir,'' Bishop said lamely. ''It's just that—''

''Yes,'' said Mrs. Pollifax, and drew a deep breath.
''You've made it quite clear, I think—both of you—but of
course I'd love to go. As soon as you said China—''

Damn, thought Bishop, *she's going to go: Carstairs'
blood pressure will be up for days, and I'll have to resort
to tranquilizers. This is always what happens after she
goes because all hell usually breaks loose around this
woman and we have to sit here in Langley Field, Virginia,
and worry about her. How could we have forgotten this?*

''Good—we did hope you'd take this on for us,'' Carstairs
was saying heartily, ''because I can't think of anyone who
would provide a better aura of—well, respectability, but at
the same time be resourceful enough to make a contact that
is *not* going to be easy. You can leave in ten days, on June
first?''

Mrs. Pollifax smiled. "You once gave me exactly one hour's notice. Yes, I can leave in ten days."

"And Cyrus Reed," put in Carstairs. "I hear that it's turned into quite a romance between you two, and that you've been seeing a great deal of each other since you met. Will he object to your doing another job for us?"

"Cyrus," she said, neatly fielding both comment and question, "is in Africa until June sixth. He left last week to visit his daughter. The daughter," she reminded them, "who was on safari with us last summer and met and married a doctor there."

Both of them nodded. In any case, thought Bishop, the question had been a mere courtesy; both he and Carstairs knew very well that Cyrus was safely out of the country and could make no objections.

"But what is it," asked Mrs. Pollifax, "that you do have in mind?"

"We'll get to it, shall we?" said Carstairs, and left his desk, moving to the opposite wall where he pulled down a large map of the People's Republic of China. "Our particular problem, as I said," he began pleasantly, "is that it's almost as impossible to get an agent into the country as it is to get someone out. Especially since the man we want to rescue—let's call him X for the moment, shall we?—is in a rather inaccessible area. Actually," he added casually, "in a labor camp."

"Labor camp!" exclaimed Mrs. Pollifax.

"Labor *reform* camp, and roughly in this area." Picking up a pencil he described a circle that enclosed a startling number of miles in the northwest corner, a region colored yellow-brown on the map, denoting desert and other inhospitable possibilities, with only the names of a few cities or towns interrupting the space.

"But that's a great deal of country," pointed out

Mrs. Pollifax, taken aback. "And you don't know exactly where?"

"Not precisely, no," said Carstairs. "That's what we hope you'll find out from the man you contact in Xian, who spent several years in that same labor reform camp. His name, by the way, is Guo Musu. He's a Buddhist, and they suffered rather extravagantly during the Cultural Revolution. Many of their temples and monasteries were taken over or destroyed, and the monks sent off to communes or labor camps, where in either case they were given massive doses of Mao's thinking . . . gems such as book learning can never be considered genuine knowledge, and how heroic it is to give oneself totally to one's Motherland—and of course to Mao. Because of this we hope he'll prove sympathetic enough to pinpoint the location of that camp for you."

"He's a barber now," put in Bishop.

Carstairs nodded. "Yes, in Xian. He also speaks enough English to communicate," he added parenthetically. "We gleaned this information from his brother, who fled China for Hong Kong, where refugees from the mainland are habitually questioned. It's the right camp—Ching Ho Forestry Camp—which means Clean Stream in English. They have a penchant for giving camps and prisons delightful names," he said dryly. "And contacting Guo Musu will be your job."

"I see," said Mrs. Pollifax, looking dazed. "But if Mr. Guo chooses not to pinpoint the location, or can't be found in Xian?"

"We're not entertaining thoughts of failure," Carstairs told her firmly. "This Mr. X has got to be found and brought out before the Russians get to him."

"Russians!" exclaimed Mrs. Pollifax.

"Yes." Leaning against the corner of his desk he said, "One of our agents who works for the Soviets—a double-agent, needless to say—has brought us information of X's existence and of the Soviets' interest in him. Before summer's end the Russians will be mounting a major undercover operation to get this chap out of China, too.''

''But—one may ask why?''

''Because our friend X knows a great deal about China's fortifications along the Russian border,'' Carstairs said. ''In fact, he designed a good share of them—the below-ground sections added in the late sixties and early seventies, at least. By our good fortune no one in the government has remembered him yet. Apparently somewhere along the way, through some error in the records or through being mistaken for a prisoner who died, our Mr. X has acquired the name and identity of another man. I don't want to confuse you with names, but if I tell you that X's true and proper name is Wang Shen, and that his current name is Wong Shen, then you can share speculations on what happened.''

Mrs. Pollifax nodded. ''I see . . . He's an engineer, then. But how did he end up in a labor camp?''

''That we don't know,'' Carstairs said. ''Some indiscretion or other, a confidence shared with the wrong person, a banned book seen in his possession—it scarcely matters; it happened to so many people during Mao's time.'' He nodded toward the map. ''What matters is this seven hundred miles of shared border between the two countries, between Russia—her former mentor and big brother, now an uneasy and threatening neighbor—and China, struggling to assert her rightful position in the world. It's worth a great deal to the Soviets to learn in precise detail what booby traps face them along that frontier—and no one in China realizes that Wang Shen, with all that information in his head, is still alive.''

''Astonishing,'' said Mrs. Pollifax, blinking at this.

''It's especially important to prevent Wang from falling

into the Russians' hands,'' went on Carstairs. ''We could, of course, notify the Chinese of the Russians' interest in the man, but frankly we're not sure what the government would do about it. He is presumably listed as a counter-revolutionary, a revisionist, a capitalist-roader, or some such, or he wouldn't be in a labor reform camp. He's also thousands of miles from Peking, in a country still heavily weighted with Mao bureaucrats. Someone just might decide that killing him would be the simplest solution.''

Mrs. Pollifax, considering this, could see his point.

''And,'' he continued, with a faint smile, ''lest you think we're being altruistic here, we'd be delighted to have a chat with Mr. Wang ourselves in the interest of preserving the balance of power on this fragile planet.'' He sighed. ''Very touchy thing, that border. Our satellite photos can't tell us very much because so many of China's defenses are underground. The Chinese military can be charmingly frank about being years behind in defense, but they can also be charmingly vague about what they have over there to hold Russia back—other than a billion people, underground shelters, and anti-aircraft on every hill, of course.''

''I begin to understand,'' said Mrs. Pollifax dryly.

''Yes. A great deal depends on China's being strong enough to keep the Russians in check. Since *we'd* never attack through Russia, it's obviously a matter of reassurance for us, but there's also the fact that if Wang is valuable enough for the Russians to want we'd like to take a whack at getting him ourselves.''

''But with difficulty,'' she pointed out.

''Good Lord, yes. Travel in China is very circumscribed. China watchers we have, and compilers of statistics, and news from any Chinese who leave by way of Canton for Hong Kong,'' he explained, ''but our Embassy people in Beijing—the new name for Peking—are still pretty much confined there, except for carefully arranged inspections of communes and factories. The country is *extremely* security conscious. The Chinese themselves can't travel at all unless they're given special permission by their units—which, when you come to think of it," he said thoughtfully, "is a damn clever way of keeping track of a billion people."

Mrs. Pollifax, frowning, said, "Then how—?"

He nodded. "Exactly. What we're up against here is China's hinterland—Xinjiang Uygur Autonomous Region, thousands of miles from any official points of entry. High mountains. Desert land that's being reclaimed by irrigation. A region of minority peoples, and X—Mr. Wang—hidden somewhere in the middle of it. Remote, to say the least."

"To say the least," murmured Mrs. Pollifax, startled.

"However, the area *is* being visited by occasional tourists now, looking for the unusual and the offbeat—always, of course, led by a China Travel Service guide, but nevertheless a pleasant way to reach the area."

"Ah," murmured Mrs. Pollifax, leaning forward now attentively.

"It's too risky, sending you and another agent together, just the two of you, with a guide. What we're putting together for June first is a small group of what are known in the tourist-agency trade as 'wait list' people. Markham Tours here is cooperating without knowing the real reason. 'Wait list' people are those who signed up too late with Markham Tours, and have been placed on a waiting list, and would be willing to forego an American tour guide with the group in order to go there. Bishop, the brochure."

Bishop stoically handed Mrs. Pollifax the glossy colorful booklet whose words he already knew by heart . . . an extraordinary tour of Marco Polo's Silk Road presented only by Markham Tours . . . archaeological sites, among them the Yunkang Caves of Datong, the Imperial Tomb in Xian of Qin Shi Huang . . .

"The Imperial Tomb of Qin Shi Huang?" gasped Mrs. Pollifax, scanning the first page. "But I've read about that—all those lifesized terra-cotta warriors and horses they found! How thrilling—and the Silk Road, too?"

"Yes," said Carstairs. "Miss Markham was one of the first to visit China when it opened up, and to arrange for visitors. This won't be one their regular tours, but they'll make the arrangements and use their considerable connections to make sure it's a bona fide sight-seeing experience for you all. What they *can't* provide at such short notice, however, is one of their own American guides to accompany you, so you'll be in the hands of a native guide, which may or may not be limiting, depending on his or her command of English."

And which, added Bishop silently, *is not at all accidental, my dear Mrs. Pollifax, no matter how contrite and apologetic Carstairs may sound.*

"I see," she said, and was silent, thinking about all that he'd said. "What occurs to me—"

"Yes?"

"What I don't understand—seeing that you're sending in an agent to find Mr. X, or Wang—is how that person will be able to smuggle Mr. X out of China and—"

"That," intervened Carstairs smoothly, "will be *our* problem."

"—and also," she added relentlessly, "how that agent will have any freedom of movement to even contact Mr. X, or Wang, especially traveling in a group and under the eyes of a government guide."

Good for you, Emily, thought Bishop, *you're getting close to the heart of the matter which is exactly why I'm having chills.* He waited patiently for Carstairs to field this with his usual tact.

"That will also be our problem," Carstairs said silkily.

"It's much safer if you know nothing about it, not even which member of your party will be the agent."

Caught off balance by this, Mrs. Pollifax gasped. "Not even who—!"

"Not until you've contacted our Buddhist chap Guo Musu in Xian," he told her firmly. "Believe me, it will be best for both of you. After all, it will be a very small tour group," he said, "and we want you to treat everyone openly and equally. After you've visited the Drum Tower in Xian—Guo's barbershop is in its shadow—your coagent will contact *you*."

Bishop watched her struggle with this, and then he turned his head and glanced at Carstairs and saw that his face had suddenly tightened. Bishop guessed what he was thinking; a moment later Carstairs proved it by saying in a surprisingly harsh voice, "There's one other instruction for you, Mrs. Pollifax. If anything unusual happens on this trip—*no matter what*—I expect you to get that tour group the hell out of the country, you understand?"

Mrs. Pollifax smiled. "Which means, of course, that you're expecting something unusual to take place?"

Carstairs gave her an unforgiving glance that was totally unlike him, and when he spoke again his voice was cool. "On the contrary, we trust it will be happily uneventful, and I believe that will be all for now, Mrs. Pollifax. Bishop can fill you in on the missing details and give you a visa application to fill out, and for this perhaps you wouldn't mind waiting out in his office for him? In the meantime we're delighted, of course, that you're taking this on."

He didn't look at all delighted; he looked rather like a man who had just swallowed a fish bone and was going to choke on it, and deep inside of him Bishop chuckled: it had finally happened, he had simply underestimated the time it would take for Carstairs to realize all the things that could go wrong, and how devilishly fond he was of Mrs. Pollifax. *Ah well,* thought Bishop cheerfully, *I've already passed through it and been inoculated, I'll just have to shore him up.*

Watching Mrs. Pollifax leave the office he waited for the door to close behind her and then he moved to a panel on the right wall with a mirror set into it. "You can come out now," he told the man who had been listening and observing from the other side.

The man who walked out to join them looked furious. "Good God," he said, "you're sending *her?* I've nothing against the woman personally, but if that's who you're sending with me into China—"

"The perfect reaction," Bishop told him imperturbably. "Do sit down and let us tell you about Mrs. Pollifax— bearing in mind, I hope, that your reactions are exactly the same that we trust China's security people will experience, too." . . .

Mrs. Pollifax, returning to New Jersey, felt that her cup was running over. It had been startling enough to fly off that morning from Teterboro in a small private plane— how surprised her neighbors would be to know of that! —but this adventure paled now beside the fact that she was actually going to visit China. She was remembering the loving report on China that she'd written in fifth grade, and the triumph of the jacket she'd given it: gold chopstick letters on dark green construction paper. Land of Pearl Buck, too, she thought dreamily—how many times had she seen the film *The Good Earth?*—and of Judge Dee mystery novels, emperors and empresses and palaces and Marco Polo and silk. They all swam together happily in her mind.

But what felt the most amazing coincidence of all was the class in Chinese art that she'd taken during the past winter; it was true that she still had a tendency to confuse the Shang, Zhou, Han, Tang, and Sung dynasties, but the professor had so frequently referred to treasures destroyed during Mao's Cultural Revolution that she had looked up a great many things about modern China as well, accumulating names like The Long March, The Great Leap Forward, the Hundred Flowers, the Cultural Revolution—which certainly appeared to be anything but kind to culture—and the Lin-Confucius Campaign. Now she was going to see China for herself, which only proved how astonishing life could be.

She happily overtipped the cab driver, and reaching the seclusion of her apartment tossed coat and hat to the couch, adjusted the curtains to give her geraniums the last of the day's sunshine, and put water on to boil for tea. Only then did she spread out the brochures and maps and *Hints to Travelers* that Bishop had given her, but it was his page of notes that interested her the most: there was the name Guo Musu to be memorized, and a tourist's map of Xian cut out of a brochure, with an X penciled in near the Drum Tower—but what, she wondered, did a Chinese barbershop look like?—and there was also a tentative list of the people who would accompany her, subject to change, Bishop had told her. She eyed these speculatively:

> Peter Fox/Connecticut
> Malcolm Styles/New York
> Jennifer A. Lobsen/Indiana
> George Westrum/Texas

Next she carefully read her travel schedule: New York to San Francisco; San Francisco to Hong Kong; overnight in Hong Kong with instructions to meet the rest of the party the next morning in the hotel's breakfast room before departure by train for Mainland China. The itinerary: Canton,

Xian, Urumchi, Lanzhou, Inner Mongolia, Datong, Taiyuan, Peking; departure from Peking for Tokyo and thence back to New York, arriving four weeks later.

While her peppermint tea steeped in its china pot she put the notes aside and glanced through the photographs in the brochure, fervently wishing she could pick up the telephone and share her excitement with Cyrus. This was very selfish of her, she admitted, because she knew that he must have been bracing himself for just this occasion. How strange it was, she mused, that Cyrus knew what even her son and her daughter didn't know: the reasons behind her small travels, the risks she met, and thinking about this she decided that in her next letter to him in Zambia she would not mention China at all; instead she'd write a separate letter that would be waiting for him on his return. This would spare him at least one or two weeks of worry—and he *would* worry, she conceded; he would know at once why she was going, and there was no way to reassure him that it was a routine assignment. "Routine?" she could hear him say. "Went to Zambia on a routine assignment, didn't you, Emily? Just to take pictures, stay out of trouble? All hell broke loose, nearly got killed, both of us, and caught an assassin. Don't mention routine to me, m'dear."

And of course at the back of her mind, not ready for admittance yet, lurked an awareness of the tension she had sensed in Bishop. She thought now, uneasily, *He knows much more than I've been told; he really hoped I'd say no*.

Lifting her eyes she glanced around at her safe, familiar apartment—at the sunlight striping the worn oriental rug, the books lining one wall, the tubs of geraniums at the window—and she remembered the number of times she'd left it without knowing what lay ahead of her, or if she would ever see it again. She said aloud, "Yet I'm here. Very definitely still here. Somehow." One had to have faith, she reminded herself, and on impulse left the brochures and walked over to her desk and removed from one of its drawers a collection of envelopes bearing colorful and exotic stamps. *Maybe I keep them for just such a moment*, she thought, knowing their contents by heart: a recent letter from her dear friend John Sebastian Farrell in Africa; a birth announcement from Colin and Sabbahat Ramsey in Turkey; a holiday message from the King of Zabya with a note from his son Hafez, and Christmas cards from Robin and Court Bourke-Jones, from the Trendafilovs, from Magda and Sir Hubert, all of them people she'd met on her adventures.

Last of all she drew out a soiled and wrinkled postcard that had reached her just last year, a card addressed to Mrs. Emily Pollifax, New Brunswick, New Jersey, the United States of America—no street address, no zip code—so that only a very enterprising postman had rescued it for her. On one side was the picture of a castle; on the opposite side the words: *You remain here still with me, Amerikanski. I do not forget. Tsanko.**

Yes, she thought softly, her life had become very rich since that day she found it so purposeless that she had tried to give it away. So many new experiences and so many new friends . . .

With a glance at the clock she put away the collection of cards and letters, and carrying her cup of tea into the bedroom she quickly changed into slacks and a shirt. An hour later she was in a back room at police headquarters, wearing her brown karate belt and making obeisances to retired police lieutenant Lorvale Brown before advanced instructions began. Presently shouts of *hi-yah* filled the air because Lorvale believed in attacking with sudden bloodcurdling shouts as well as a slice of the hand.

**The Elusive Mrs. Pollifax*

The next day Bishop called and told her to add two more names to the tour group, that of Iris Damson of Oklahoma, and Joseph P. Forbes from Illionis.

"Is he my coagent?" she blithely inquired. "Or she?"

He said with equal cheerfulness, "I'm told it's raining today in Hong Kong."

"Then may I ask instead—now that I've had more time to go over the list you gave me—why I'm to carry with me four pounds of chocolate, two pairs of thermal socks, and such an incredible supply of vitamin pills and dried fruits?"

"It's just a sneaky way to keep you from taking too many clothes," he told her. "Now don't you think you've asked enough questions?"

"Obviously," she said, and rang off.

During the next nine days Mrs. Pollifax addressed her Garden Club on The Care and Feeding of Geraniums, including their propagation from seed, studied maps and old *National Geographics*, bought a simple Chinese phrase book for the traveler, and began taking malaria tablets. She invested in a rough straw hat with a swashbuckling brim, notified children and friends of her departure, wrote several newsy letters to Cyrus in Africa, and a separate one to his home in Connecticut explaining that she was off to the Orient to do a very small job—nothing worrisome at all—for Carstairs. And on June first she flew off to Hong Kong for her great adventure—in China.

𝖽𝖽𝖽𝖽𝖽𝖽𝖽𝖽𝖽𝖽𝖽𝖽𝖽𝖽𝖽𝖽𝖽𝖽𝖽𝖽𝖽 **2**

Mrs. Pollifax picked up a spoon from the dazzling white tablecloth and beamed at the waiter who was filling her coffee cup. "Thank you," she said, glancing down at a plate that she had heaped with papaya and watermelon from the buffet, and as he left she thought happily, *It's begun, I'm here—and in only a few more hours I'll be entering China.*

She had arrived in Hong Kong the night before, after what seemed like days of travel, and her first glimpse of the Orient had been deeply satisfying. The plane had begun its descent over a fairyland harbor of boats outlined in delicate-colored lights; the shapes of mountains had drifted past the window, now and then exposing clusters of tiny white lights at their base—villages, presumably—before

17

the harbor suddenly reappeared, enchantingly toylike from the sky. There had been a young woman to meet her at the Kai Tak air terminal, and this had also been a pleasant surprise: a representative of Markham Tours who introduced herself as Miss Chu, efficiently bundled both her and her suitcase into a car, and told her that she would personally appear in the hotel lobby at eleven the next morning to introduce them all to Mr. Li, their China Travel Service guide. It had been very soothing to be under the protective wing of Markham Tours because Mrs. Pollifax's major concern had been to find a bed and sleep in it for as long as possible. Two nights in the air—her body did not yield itself happily to plane seats—had reduced her senses to a state of numbness; after flying across the United States, and then across the Pacific, she felt that nothing could excite her except bed.

It was different this morning after ten hours of sleep; she looked upon the exotic scene around her with eager interest: at the fresh flowers encircling the hotel's buffet, at the refreshingly novel Asian faces. But there was one English or American face among them: she found herself exchanging glances with a sullen-looking young man of college age seated alone at a table nearby. The fact that he did not return her smile but only glowered back at her did not dismay her at all. She felt that she loved everyone this morning, even Sullen Young Men; a recovery from exhaustion tended to have this effect upon her.

Seeing that it was nearly eight o'clock she removed from her pocket the red, white, and blue ribbon that Miss Chu had given her last night, and pinned it to the collar of her shirt for identification purposes. This action appeared to catch the eye of a bearded, stocky man just entering the restaurant, and he changed his course to head for her table against the wall.

"Good morning," he said, arriving beside her to extend

his hand. "Glad to see I'm not the first—my name's Joe Forbes."

It was on the tip of her tongue to blurt out, ah yes, the newcomer to the list, but she bit back her words just in time. "How do you do, and I'm Emily Pollifax," she said, smiling up at him as she clasped the proffered hand.

He certainly seemed likable: the two most noticeable features about him were his bristling beard and an amiable air of being at ease. He was strongly built, not tall but very fit, with a pleasant face. The brown beard was neatly trimmed and flecked with gray. His receding brown hair gave him a high forehead with only a few frown lines etched between the brows. He looked about forty, a seasoned traveler, dressed casually in a black turtleneck under a brown zip-up jacket, and corduroys and work boots. He placed a small duffle bag and a Chinese-American dictionary on a chair beside her, and with a nod at the book and a sleepy smile explained, "I'm learning Mandarin. You'll take care of these for me?"

"Of course," she told him, and watched him stroll toward the buffet, feeling very pleased about this Joseph Forbes who had made such a late appearance on the tour list, and who looked very capable and reassuring if he should turn out to be her coagent. She realized, too, that she'd forgotten the thrill of being out in the world—how small and insulated her corner of New Jersey looked from Hong Kong, crossroad of the Orient! She took another bite of papaya and:

"Oh!" cried a voice beside her. "I've found you! I'm Iris Damson!"

Startled, Mrs. Pollifax turned and looked up at the woman standing over her—looked up and smiled, and there was something about Iris Damson to make anyone's smile especially warm. She was tall and lanky and awkward, in her early thirties, perhaps, with a great deal of shoulder-

length brown hair which, in spite of being tucked behind
her ears, kept falling forward which led to still more
awkward gestures as she pushed it back. Her clothes—*oh
dear*, thought Mrs. Pollifax, *how totally and horribly wrong
for her:* a fussy summer cocktail dress with huge white
polka dots on black cotton and everything she wore
shiny-new, right down to the brilliant white purse that she
clutched in one hand. Yet there was something oddly
endearing about the effect. *She looks as if she's arrived at
a party*, thought Mrs. Pollifax. Her face was thin, with
both the jaw and nose a shade too long, but her smile was
radiant and exuded joy at being here, at having found Mrs.
Pollifax, at having found Hong Kong; it was like being
struck by a bolt of sunshine.

"I'm delighted to meet you and I'm Emily Pollifax,"
she told Iris warmly.

Iris Damson found the edge of a chair and perched on it,
then abruptly jumped up, gasping, "It's buffet? Oh, I
didn't notice." Snatching up her purse she swept a drinking glass to the floor, turned scarlet, and immediately
disappeared under the table.

Before Mrs. Pollifax could rush to her aid or soothe her
she became aware that someone else had stopped beside the
table, and half out of her chair she looked up to find a tall,
suave man at her elbow. "Oh," she gasped, feeling that
Iris' confusion had become infectious. "How do you do,
are you one of us, too?"

At that same moment Iris' head appeared above the
snowy white tablecloth and the man, startled, said in an
amused voice, "Well, hello—have you been there long?"

Iris Damson unwound herself to her full height, which
nearly equaled the man's, extended a thin arm, fervently
shook his hand, gasped, "It's *buffet*," and fled.

The man calmly sat down next to Mrs. Pollifax, his

calmness a welcome antidote. "I'm Malcolm Styles," he told her, "and you?"

"Emily Pollifax."

"Thank you. And the young woman who—er—jumps out from under tables?"

Mrs. Pollifax smiled. "That was Iris Damson, pursuing a water glass."

A waiter appeared at his elbow, saying, "Coffee, sir?"

"Love some," he said, and as the waiter left he lifted the cup to his lips and over its rim gave Mrs. Pollifax the same frank appraisal that she was giving him.

She reflected that he was precisely the sort of man that a waiter *would* hurry to wait on, her own coffee having arrived much later, and without any sense of betrayal she put aside Joe Forbes and substituted Malcolm Styles because she thought that if Malcolm Styles was not a spy, he ought to be. He looked like a male model, or the star of any Hollywood spy film, or at the very least the head of some spectacularly successful computer firm. It was not just the flawlessly cut business suit, it was that thick black guardsman's moustache and the quizzical dark eyes that also, she realized, looked extraordinarily kind. One brow was tilting up a little now as he looked at her with amusement, while the moustache followed the tilt very becomingly—oh, charming indeed—as he smiled. If she herself had unnerved Iris, thought Mrs. Pollifax, then Malcolm Styles was surely going to chronically shatter Iris's poise. She smiled back at him, genuinely liking him for the kindness in his eyes.

"Finished inspection?" he asked, amused.

She laughed. "A very thorough one, wasn't it? I think you're very elegant."

His smile deepened. "Presently I'll be wearing a very red noisy sport shirt—"

In which, thought Mrs. Pollifax, *you will look equally distinguished, let us not kid ourselves.*

"—because I've only flown in this morning after a business stopover in Tokyo. And now if breakfast is buffet—as I have been told in no uncertain terms," he said dryly, "I hope you'll excuse me?"

"Yes, of course," she told him, and watched him stroll toward the buffet, pick up a tray and manage to look both friendly and unapproachable at the same time. She wondered who would appear next, thinking how much like the first act of a play this was becoming, with each person arriving singly, and on cue. She looked up from her coffee to see a young girl approaching with a red, white, and blue ribbon pinned to her collar, but her analogy was upset when the girl turned and spoke to the older man behind her. *Not* singly, amended Mrs. Pollifax, and waited.

"Are you China?" the girl asked, coming to her table and pointing to her identical ribbon. She had a pert young face, very friendly and gamine, almost overwhelmed by huge round glasses that made her face look even smaller; her upper lip was *retroussée*, not quite meeting the lower one and exposing square white teeth. She wore a purple shirt and pink cotton skirt that emphasized her dark hair and fresh complexion. "I'm Jenny," she said. "Jenny Lobsen." Glancing over her shoulder she added, "And this is George Westrum."

Mrs. Pollifax stood up to shake hands this time. "Hello to both of you. You're traveling together?"

Jenny laughed and vigorously shook her head. "Oh no, we spotted each other's ribbons in the lobby at six o'clock this morning, I guess we're both still on San Francisco time. So we went walking. It was great—we saw people practicing Tai Chi in the park."

Mrs. Pollifax extended her hand to George Westrum, amused by the difference in temperament between him and

Jenny. Although he wore a boyish cap tilted back on his head, George Westrum was a very dour-looking man in his fifties. His face was taciturn and weathered, with a tight mouth that looked like a purse snapped shut forever, yet as he gripped her hand and looked squarely at her Mrs. Pollifax swore that she saw a twinkle in the man's eye.

"Just George will do," he said.

A twinkle, a baseball cap, and a tight mouth—very interesting, she thought. "I'm Emily Pollifax," she told them, and mentally running over Bishop's list she added, "And now we're all here except for one person."

At that moment she became aware that Sullen Young Man from the nearby table had risen and was strolling toward them, still looking as if he preferred to be elsewhere, and also rather out of place in his ancient faded jeans and jogging shoes. Reaching them he said, "I've had my breakfast and I'm just leaving—I'm Peter Fox." He looked at each of them one by one, nodded, added, "See you later," and before anyone could speak he walked out of the breakfast room.

So much for him, thought Mrs. Pollifax, startled, as she gazed after him. She wondered whether his hostility was going to infect and effect the others; she thought, too, how unfriendly it was of him to have sat nearby for so long, watching but without declaring himself.

But there was research to be done on all of them, she remembered, and with a glance at her watch she excused herself, secure in the knowledge that at least she had met her six tour companions, however superficially. At the top of her research list, however, she now placed Peter Fox. Assignment aside, she found that she was intensely curious as to what had brought him here, and apparently so unwillingly.

*   *   *

Huge crowds surrounded the railway station, encircling it in lines ten deep until it looked, said George Westrum, exactly like a baseball stadium at World Series time besieged by eager fans. With Miss Chu and Mr. Li to run interference, they made their way through line after line to a smaller queue inside the building, where they waited with families gripping small portable fans in one hand and food packages in string bags in the other: visitors to Canton, bearing gifts to relatives.

"This must be first class," murmured George Westrum, standing just behind her.

"In a classless society?" said Mrs. Pollifax in amazement.

Again she surprised that twinkle. "It's a matter of semantics," he said. "They call them soft seats, as against the hard seats for the masses out there."

"You've visited China before, then?"

"I read a lot," he said simply.

She smiled at him. "And what do you think of our newly met China guide?"

"Mr. Li? Young and very organized," he said. "Put him in Western clothes and he'd be a junior executive anywhere. IBM, probably."

She laughed. In spite of Mr. Li's modest attire it was exactly that executive quality, with its sense of coiled energy, that had first struck her on meeting him, too. Or perhaps his attire wasn't modest at all, she thought, as she glanced around and compared him with the other Chinese waiting in line, for his sandals were of leather, not plastic; she had already glimpsed black silk socks with tiny clocks on them, and he wore a digital watch on his wrist. She only wished that she could be more confident about his English, which was spoken with enthusiasm at a reckless speed and with an explosive laugh at the end of each statement.

The crowd suddenly began to move and they achieved

the train at last, said good-bye to Miss Chu, and climbed aboard the appointed car that would take them across the Lo Wu bridge into Mainland China. Mrs. Pollifax, entering the car last of all, chose to sit next to Peter Fox, from whom she received a swift, bored glance. Paying this no attention she gazed around in awe at the starched lace curtains at each window of the railway car, and the pale blue decor. Everything was immaculate; in fact no sooner were they all seated than a young woman hurried out from some inner sanctum to run a damp floor mop up and down the aisle and erase every hint of traffic. Music began; a small TV screen over the door sprang to life and as the train began to move, so did figures on the screen: a happy smiling young woman sang a Chinese song in a strident singsong voice; a handsome young man joined her and with large gestures and an even happier smile reinforced the suggestion of total bliss in Mainland China. Mrs. Pollifax watched in fascination, and then her attention moved past Peter Fox's impassive profile to the lush green countryside sliding past the window.

Eventually the stoniness of that profile challenged her. "Excited?" she asked Peter Fox, not without irony.

He turned and gave her a measuring glance. "Half and half," he said with a shrug.

Being direct by nature she refused such tiresome ambiguousness. "What made you come, then?" she asked. "What made you choose China?"

"I didn't," he said.

Mrs. Pollifax began to feel amused by this conversation. "I thought you seemed a little martyred," she said, warming to the game. "Of course my next question—naturally—is just why and what—"

But apparently he was not playing games. "I didn't mean to seem martyred," he said, with deadly seriousness and a scowl. "It's just I'm still making up my mind

whether I'll like it. It's a college graduation present from
my grandmother.''

"Ah," said Mrs. Pollifax. "It was her idea then, China?"

He nodded. "She was born here—spent the first thirteen
years of her life in China, so China it had to be.''

"For you but not for *her?*"

He said with a shrug, "Well, she's been in a wheelchair
the last eight years.''

"Oh, I see. I'm sorry. So you had no choice," she said,
nodding, and noticed how white his skin was at close
quarters. A pair of too-heavy dark eyebrows emphasized
this pallor, and when they drew together in a frown—as
they were doing now—they dominated his face, with its
high cheekbones and stubborn jaw.

"Well—since I've never traveled before," he said with
another shrug, "China just seems a freaky place to start. I
mean, I've never traveled even in the United States, let
alone Europe where everyone seems to begin. I suppose
you've been to Europe?" he asked suspiciously.

"Oh, here and there," she said vaguely, and watching
that impassive face she asked on impulse, "Don't you ever
smile?''

He turned and gave her such a suddenly shrewd and
thoughtful look that she was taken aback; she realized that
in some way she was amusing *him*. "That goes with it?"
he asked.

Oh, very hostile, she thought. "I was also wondering
how old you are," she told him with a smile. "A second
impertinent question for you.''

"Twenty-two," he said dryly.

In the seat ahead of them Malcolm Styles turned and
said, "I heard that, and I'm sitting with Jenny here, who's
twenty-five. Shall we change seats and let the infants have
a go at each other?''

Jenny's piquant face surfaced beside his. "Infants!" she

protested. "Why don't we just turn the seats and face each other?"

"You'll miss the scenery."

"We can see it backwards for a while. Where was your grandmother born in China, Peter?"

He reached into his duffle bag and brought out a small wrinkled map. "We go near it toward the end of the tour. I was told the guide could arrange a side trip so I can take pictures. A little village outside Datong," he said, handing her the map and pointing. "Not too far from Beijing."

Malcolm said gently, "I hope we can all see it. What was it like in those days?"

"Warlords," said Peter, and nodded. "Yeah, I guess it'll be interesting to see what's happened since then; it sure beats reading about it. Her father was a doctor-missionary, and I guess they saw terrible things while they were there. Droughts. Famine. Confiscatory taxes. Disease."

"I hear even flies have been eliminated now," said Malcolm, "although not the occasional drought, flood, and earthquake, unfortunately. What about you, Jenny?" he asked. "Why China?"

Jenny beamed at him. "Well, I'd done enough back-packing through Europe—sorry, Peter," she said, laughing at him, "and China it had to be, even if I had to borrow half the money to get here, which I did, because second-grade teachers aren't exactly rich. Which is what I am," she explained with a lively gesture. "Not rich but a second-grade teacher. There's such a strong pull in me toward China that I just have to have been Chinese in a past life."

"The Empress of course," said Peter, and suddenly grinned at her, those relentless black brows lifting to wipe away several years and make him a believable twenty-two-year-old.

"A smile!" exclaimed Malcolm, with a humorous glance at Mrs. Pollifax.

"I see it," she said, smiling back at him. "Beautiful."

With the arrival of Peter's first smile came the young woman with mop and pail again, to walk up and down and leave glistening streaks of water behind her. Mrs. Pollifax's gaze moved beyond her to the window: to rice paddies with tender green shoots springing out of the water, a water buffalo plodding along a path behind an old woman, piles of mud-and-straw bricks and trimmed logs, and a house on stilts. She heard Jenny say, "Mr. Styles—"

"Malcolm, please."

"Okay. Malcolm, you haven't said what you do when you're not traveling."

Mrs. Pollifax watched the black guardsman's moustache tilt down as the brows rose humorously. "Now that will have to wait," he told her lightly, "because it's time for me to check out the men's room—if my walking up the aisle doesn't bring out that mop again."

Mrs. Pollifax gave him a thoughtful glance as he left, thinking how adroitly he'd sidestepped answering Jenny when it would have needed only a second to say *I'm in business, theater, or advertising.* She'd not expected him to be evasive; his voice had been quietly dismissing, and there was no overlooking his well-timed retreat. She wondered what he wanted to conceal and why he wasn't ready for that question. Perhaps, she speculated, he was taking refuge in the men's room to decide just what he did do when he was not traveling.

Or perhaps she was looking much too hard for her coagent, except that she felt it ridiculous that she not know.

The train was slowing. Joe Forbes strolled up the aisle and called out to them, "Mr. Li says we're reaching the border now, and box lunches for us in half an hour."

At once cameras were unfurled and the buffs sprang to their feet, everyone except Mrs. Pollifax and Iris, who remained seated up front. Gazing out the window she thought again, *So many people!* They stood in queues, waiting to board the rear cars that George Westrum had called hard seats, and the lines were serpentine: men and women in simple cotton clothes holding bundles and waiting, among them soldiers in khaki with red stars on their caps, and behind them a series of shabby buildings and the outline of low green hills.

Mrs. Pollifax left her seat and walked down the aisle to join Iris. "Not taking pictures, I see."

Iris looked up, startled. "Oh I'll take a few later, just for me." She smiled. "No matter what I do, though, they come out weird. Heads chopped off, and that sort of thing." With a gesture toward the window she said, "I was just thinking what my friend Suzie would say about all those huts and rice paddies we passed. Suzie loves glamour; she'd say, 'You're spending all that money to fly halfway around the world and see *this?*' "

Mrs. Pollifax smiled. "I suppose if you chose one of the city tours—Shanghai especially—you'd find nightlife and glamour. Were you tempted?"

"Cities are what I know best," Iris said ruefully. "But," she added firmly, "I wanted something different."

Mrs. Pollifax nodded. "I think you found it."

Iris grinned back at her. "I think so, too." She turned in her seat to face her. "Look, Mrs.—it's Pollifax, isn't it? This dress—it's no good, is it."

"No," said Mrs. Pollifax calmly.

"Damn," Iris said without rancor, "I knew I shouldn't trust Suzie. She's a go-go dancer," she explained, "and the only person I know who's traveled. Once to the Caribbean and once to Bermuda, so I let her choose for me."

"I've never met a go-go dancer," Mrs. Pollifax said thoughtfully.

"Really?" Iris bestowed her large radiant smile on her. "I should keep my mouth shut, but since you've never met one I'll tell you that you're talking to one now. You wouldn't believe it, would you, with me being so clumsy, but when I dance I'm not. And how else would I know Suzie?" she asked candidly. "I did it full time for three years, and then when I started college I worked part time until I finished college last month."

"College last month," repeated Mrs. Pollifax, and realized that her instincts had been sound and that Iris was going to have ever-widening dimensions.

"Began college at twenty-eight," Iris said triumphantly. "Took a high-school-equivalency test and just started because I never did finish high school. Maybe it's a college nobody's heard of, but it was just right for me. And I happened to take a year's course on China," she added, "and was the only person in the class to get an A. So I decided you could have Paris and London, I was going to come to China. Except I *told* Suzie there'd be no cocktail parties or men, but she said, 'What's a trip without cocktail parties and men?' "

"What indeed," said Mrs. Pollifax, fascinated.

"So I reminded her men are what I don't need, having been married often enough, but Suzie—"

"Often enough?" echoed Mrs. Pollifax, regarding her with some awe.

Iris nodded. "At sixteen to a cowboy—that was Mike—and then to Stanley, who turned out to be a crook, and then to Orris. *He* struck oil, which is when he decided he was too good for me. He was nice, though, he gave me a really fair shake when he left, and I may be dumb about clothes but not about money. That's when I decided I'd had enough, though, and it was time to change my life."

"Yes," said Mrs. Pollifax, and waited.

"I mean," Iris went on eagerly, "we let men define who we are, right? That's Women's Lib. I went to some of the meetings at college and I could see how it had been with me. For Mike I ate beans and franks all the time and was a cocktail waitress. For Stanley I learned how to keep my mouth shut about his shady deals—'button up,' he was always growling. For Orris I lived in a trailer on the oil fields and was a go-go dancer until he struck it rich. And you know what?" she added, leaning forward and shoving back her mane of hair, "I did it all to please *them,* not me."

"I see exactly what you mean," said Mrs. Pollifax, admiring the passion of Iris' discoveries.

"Except now I've let Suzie influence me," she said, glancing ruefully down at the huge polka dots and stiff white collar. "What do I do? Will there be clothes in Canton, do you think?"

"Chinese clothes."

Iris scowled. "I'm too big, I'm nearly six feet tall."

"Didn't you bring anything to—well, relax in?"

"I stuck in a pair of old jeans at the last minute—something old and something blue," she said wryly. "In case I had a chance to ride horseback or something. And a denim shirt."

"Wear them," Mrs. Pollifax told her firmly.

Iris looked startled. "But Jenny's in that pretty little skirt and blouse, and look at you in—"

Mrs. Pollifax shook her head. "Wear them."

Iris sighed. "Gosh, the money I spent on all this stuff, enough to keep Vogue Boutique in business a whole year, I swear."

"You'll look splendid in jeans," said Mrs. Pollifax, paying this no attention. "Be yourself."

Iris considered this and sighed again. "There it is again,

the hardest thing of all, don't you think? Being yourself? But if I should blossom out in my jeans tomorrow would you stick near me?''

''For the initial impact, yes, but after that you're on your own.''

Iris grinned. ''You're really nice. I thought when I first saw you, oh boy *she'll* be the one to cold-shoulder me—I mean, when I first saw you, before I spoke to you. And here I end up telling you the story of my life.''

''Stanley,'' said Mrs. Pollifax, ''would have told you to 'button up'?''

Iris laughed her joyous laugh. ''You sure listened if you remember *that*. Oh-oh, here comes Mr. Forbes again. He's certainly no talker, he just keeps studying that Chinese dictionary of his.''

''Yes, but I took his seat and I'll let him have it back now,'' Mrs. Pollifax told her. ''I'll see you later, Iris.''

As the others streamed back into the car the train lurched and then began to move, and Mr. Li appeared carrying a carton of box lunches for them. A moment later the railway station and the border were behind them, and Mrs. Pollifax thought, *We're now in Mainland China. It begins at last.*

3

THEY DINED LATE THAT AFTERNOON IN THE GUANGZHOU Restaurant, just off the train and in another world. Their number had been increased by one, the local Guangzhou, or Canton guide who explained that the hotel was so far out of town that they must have their Chinese banquet now. The man's name was Tung, and Mrs. Pollifax began to understand now that only Mr. Li was to be permanent and *theirs;* the others would come and go, with names like Chu and Tung, leaving only vague impressions behind.

In any case, Mrs. Pollifax felt that her sense of inner time was still so confused that a banquet in late afternoon could scarcely be more difficult than breakfast at night over the Pacific. They were here, very definitely in China, on the second floor of a huge old wooden building in a room filled with large round tables, only one of which was occupied by a family of Chinese who ate and talked with enthusiasm in a far corner: a wedding party, explained Mr. Li.

With her chopsticks Mrs. Pollifax lifted a slice of sugared tomato toward her mouth and experienced triumph at its arrival. From where she sat she could look out across the restaurant's courtyard and see a line of clothes hung on a rope stretched from eave to eave: an assortment of grays, dull blues, and greens. She decided that it was probably not someone's laundry because the wide street outside had been lined with just such clothing too, hung like banners from every apartment above the street floor. Presumably it was an efficient solution to a lack of closet space, and remembering her own crowded closets at home she pondered the effect on her neighbors if she did this at the Hemlock Arms.

Mr. Li, seated beside her, chose this moment to announce, "It is important there be a leader to this group. You are oldest, Mrs. Pollifax, you will please be leader?"

Mrs. Pollifax, glancing around, said doubtfully, "I'm the oldest, yes, but I wonder if perhaps—" She stopped, aware that Iris' eyes were growing huge with alarm at the thought of her deferring to a man and betraying The Cause. She wondered if later it would prove convenient or inconvenient to be a leader, and Carstairs' words drifted back to her: *if anything unusual happens—if anything goes wrong—get that group the hell out of China.* Possibly, she decided, it might prove convenient. "Yes of course," she said, and smiled demurely at Iris across the table.

Mr. Li laughed merrily. "Good-okay! You can find for me out of each person what they most want to see. For the arrangements. We cannot promise them, it is the local guides who decide, but I struggle for you."

"Yes," said Mrs. Pollifax, and decided not to mention the Drum Tower in Xian just yet.

"For tomorrow," said Mr. Li, "Mr. Tung has arranged—" He bent his ear to Mr. Tung and surfaced, nodding. "We visit Dr. Sun Yet-sen Memorial Hall, the panda at the zoo, various other stops, and late in afternoon departure to Xian."

"The beginning of the Silk Road," pointed out Malcolm, nodding.

George Westrum, on her left, said gruffly, "For myself, I'll say right now that I want to see their farms, and the equipment they have. That'll be communes, of course."

"I'll make a note of that," she told him. "You're a farmer, George?"

"Have a few acres," he said.

Mrs. Pollifax gave him an exasperated glance. She had wrested words out of young Peter, and had witnessed Malcolm's evasiveness, and she was bored with all this modesty. She asked bluntly, "How many?"

"Several thousand," he admitted.

"Cows, horses, sheep, or grain?" she shot back.

"Beef cattle. And oil."

"Aha!"

He nodded. "A surprise to me, that oil," he said. "Retired early from government work—"

"Government work?"

"Yes, and bought a ranch, expecting to raise cattle, not oil. That young lady I saw you talking to on the train," he said casually, with a not-so-casual glance across the table at Iris. "She Miss or Mrs. Damson?"

Mrs. Pollifax's *aha* was silent this time. "I haven't the slightest idea," she told him cheerfully, "except that I do know she's not married now. Is this a thousand-year-old egg?" she asked, turning to Mr. Li.

"Oh yes, but *not* a thousand years old," he said with his quick smile and another merry laugh.

"It tastes like egg, it just looks rather odd, as if it had been left out of the refrigerator too long."

Jenny said, "I believe they're soaked in brine or something, and buried in the earth."

"The food's coming with frightening speed now," pointed out Malcolm across the table as the waiter brought still another platter to the table. "Sweet and sour something," he announced, spearing a piece between chopsticks and delivering it to his mouth before passing it on. "How many meals will be Chinese on our trip?"

"It is good, you all using chopsticks," said Mr. Li. "Very good. You, Mr. Fox—press fingers a little higher," he told Peter, receiving a hostile glance in return. "The food? After tomorrow no Western food."

"Not even breakfast?" gasped Jenny.

"Chinese breakfast."

"What fun," cried Iris with a radiant smile.

"I've been studying Chinese this last year," Joe Forbes told him across the table. "I'd like to try it out on you now and then. For instance, would I be called a *da bi zi?*"

Both Mr. Li and Mr. Tung burst out laughing. "*Xiao hua,*" cried Mr. Li enthusiastically.

"Meaning what?" asked Jenny.

Joe Forbes said, "I *hope* I asked if I'd be called a 'long nose' among the Chinese—except it's so damn easy to get the tones wrong. Did I?"

"You did, yes," Mr. Tung assured him, "and Comrade Li said *Xiao hua,* meaning 'a joke'!"

"Surely we're called round eyes, not long noses," asked Malcolm.

"Anyway not foreign devils anymore," contributed Jenny.

"Capitalist-roaders?" suggested Iris, grinning.

Mr. Tung gave an embarrassed laugh. Mr. Li lifted his

glass of pale orange soda pop and said, "Let us toast to
Chinese-American friendship!"

Mrs. Pollifax raised her own glass of soda. The others
lifted their glasses of Chinese beer, which she promised
herself she would try the next day, since water was ad-
vised against, the tea extremely weak, and the soda tasted
rather like flavored water. In the meantime she waited to
ask George Westrum just what his government service
might have been. He was a silent man but he talked well
when he did speak; his face was expressionless, even
harsh, but there was that occasional twinkle of humor that
suggested other dimensions. He must certainly have retired
early—as CIA men often did, Bishop had told her—because
he looked to be still in his fifties, and he was obviously
strong. She felt that he was noticing everyone and
everything—watching and alert—and she was amused that
he had especially noticed Iris.

But there was no opportunity to question George Westrum
further. Mr. Li, pleased that Forbes was learning Mandarin,
at once grasped the chance to practice his English, and
their exchange of words occupied the others. "Yes, I teach
history," Forbes was saying, "in a small Midwestern
university." He was smiling but Mrs. Pollifax realized that
actually he did not smile all the time, it was merely an
illusion caused by the arrangement of his features, but
definitely smiling now, she could see the difference.

"Professor?" said Iris, and made a startled gesture that
struck a nearby bottle of beer and sent it rolling off the
table. Iris turned scarlet. "Oh," she gasped. "Oh I'm
terrible sorry." She dropped her napkin and started after
it.

Malcolm placed a firm hand on her arm. "Please," he
said with a smile. "Not again. Let me do the honors this
time."

"Oh! Oh thank you," said Iris, her cheeks burning.

But a waiter had rushed to the table to wipe up the spilled beer, just as another waiter arrived bearing a huge soup tureen. "Now that looks too heavy for Iris to tip over," Jenny said, with a laugh.

"I understand soup means the end of a meal in your country," Joe Forbes put in. "In America we have it first, you know."

Mr. Tung looked appalled.

"We feel," explained Mr. Li gently, "that it belongs at the end. To settle the dinner."

"And don't forget," Malcolm pointed out, "the Chinese gave us silk, printing, gunpowder, and porcelain among other things."

"But obviously not the idea of soup to end a meal," added Jenny.

Mrs. Pollifax put down her chopsticks. It had been a lavish dinner—melons, rice, pork, shrimp, eggs, tomatoes, more courses than she could count—but she was glad to see it ending. *It's been a long day,* she thought, *and I miss Cyrus . . . I can't go through China missing Cyrus, I have work to do. I haven't managed Yoga for three days, perhaps that's it.*

They rose from the table, descended dusty wooden stairs, and left the restaurant to be assaulted by the life outside. Mrs. Pollifax revived at once and looked around her with pleasure: at the broad street dense with people and bicycles, at children stopping to stare at them shyly and then smile. Off to one side she saw a line of stalls piled high with shirts, plastic sandals, bananas, sunflower seeds, and nuts. A woman and child sat patiently beside a very small table, waiting to sell a few bottles of garishly bright orange soda pop. Across the street small huts had been squeezed on top of the roof of a long cement building from which the paint was peeling. Flowers in pots stood on ledges, or flowed down from roof dwellings and apartments to overhang the street. The colors were muted, except for the flowers and the flash of an occasional red shirt. Even the sounds were muted: the persistent ringing of bicycle bells—there were no cars—and the shuffle of feet. It was approaching dusk, and the day's heat had turned into a warmth that mingled pleasantly with the smells of cooking food. *This is more like it*, thought Mrs. Pollifax, drinking in the smells and sights, and it was with reluctance that she climbed back into the minibus.

This time it was Malcolm Styles who took the seat next to her. As he leaned over to place his small travel kit under the seat a pocket notebook fell out of his pocket and dropped into her lap. She picked it up and handed it back to him, but a solitary sheet of paper had escaped and settled into a niche beside the window. Retrieving this she glanced at it and gasped, "But how lovely!"

It was a sketch—a line-drawing in pen and ink—of a Chinese child, no more than a quick sketch but with lines so fluid and joyful that it staggered her with its delicacy, its aliveness. She looked at Malcolm with amazement. "You're an artist!"

His grin was rueful, those thick brows drawing together deprecatingly. "Of a sort."

"Stop being modest," she told him sternly. "What do you *do* with a gift like this?"

His eyes smiled at her. "I'm not at all modest," he told her. "Really I'm not. I just feel very uncomfortable when people learn that I wrote and illustrated the Tiny Tot series, and am now the author of the Doctor Styles' picture books, and—"

"The Doctor Styles' books!" she exclaimed. "Good heavens, my grandchild adores them, I sent him one at Christmas and—but that means you also wrote *The Boy Who Walked Into a Rainbow?*"

He nodded. "That's me."

She gazed at him incredulously. "I thought you were an actor or a fervent businessman," she told him. "Or a male model—you know, distinguished gentleman who drinks only the best sherry or stands beside a Rolls-Royce smoking a briar pipe and looking owlish."

"With attaché case?" he asked interestedly.

"Oh, *welded* to one," she told him.

He nodded. "Then you can understand the shock when people discover that I live in a world inhabited by rabbits that talk and mice who rescue small boys."

"Well—yes," she admitted, smiling. "Yes, that could be a shock."

"It is," he assured her. "Usually there's an instinctive withdrawal, then a look of suspicion, followed by a hearty 'By Jove that's nice,' and a very hasty retreat. I must say you've taken it rather well, though."

"Not a great deal surprises me," admitted Mrs. Pollifax. "Not anymore, at least. It must surely make for a very good life?"

"Oh yes I'm very fortunate," he said lightly. "I do only one book a year now, and that leaves six months for travel or for anything else that appeals."

Six months, she mused, turning this over in her mind; yes there were certain possibilities there, and his books made for wonderful cover. "Are you hoping for a book from this trip?"

He said softly, "Oh I think not, but it will refresh me. I'm looking forward intensely to the Qin Shi Huang Tombs—"

"Oh yes!"

"—and the museums and temples. And sketching, of course."

They had been driving through darkening streets—there

were no street lights—and now as night arrived there were only dim electric lights shining yellow in the apartments along the streets. Glancing up she could look into the windows and see a single feeble bulb suspended from the ceiling, see the dark silhouette of a man standing at a window peering out, glimpse a face seated at a table reading, the light etching the face in chiaroscuro. Hong Kong's fluorescent lights had been stark clear white; here the color was a yellow that barely illuminated the dark caves of rooms.

"Surely those can't be more than twenty-watt bulbs?" she murmured to Malcolm, pointing.

"Twenty-five at most," he said.

Huge dark China, she thought, moved by the silence, the absence of cars, and the darkness.

The buildings thinned until the headlights of the bus picked out mud-brick walls, then lines of trees with only a solitary light to be seen at a distance—a commune, perhaps—and then at last the bus turned down a graveled road that ran through a thinly wooded area, lights gleamed ahead, and they drew up before a huge, raw, half-finished modern building.

"I hope," said Mrs. Pollifax with feeling, "our hotels aren't always going to be *this* far out of town."

"The question being," Malcolm said, extending a hand to her, "whether they're trying to keep us from meeting the people, or the people from meeting us."

They walked into a huge echoing lobby that was almost a parody of contempory architecture: a few self-consciously Danish chairs, a very Art Deco cobblestone fish pond, with a fountain springing out of its base. They were the only people in the cavernous lobby except for a young woman behind a desk who passed out room keys to them.

"Bags outside rooms at half-past seven," said Mr. Li. "We do not return here to the hotel tomorrow, remember."

"It would take hours to get back here anyway," commented Iris, and received an answering smile from George Westrum.

Mrs. Pollifax entered room 217, found it bland but comfortable, with hot water running from its sink taps, and promptly ran a bath and climbed into it. She carried with her a book on China's history to read, but she did not read it. She was too busy wondering instead what lay ahead of her in this vast country; she wondered what the others were thinking, and who among them was thinking ahead to Xian, and then to Xinjiang Province lying to the north of them. She was remembering, too, the strange assortment of items that she'd brought into China with her, the stores of vitamin pills and dried fruit, the thermal socks, and chocolate. She remembered Carstairs saying, "It's almost as impossible to get an agent into China as it is to get a man out of China."

Out of China . . . this was the question that had occurred and reoccurred to her before her departure; how *did* they plan to get X out of China? It was a question that had sent her to the very good topographical map in her encyclopedia, and the result had chilled her because Xinjiang Province, thousands of miles from the sea, bordered Tibet and Pakistan and Afghanistan, its desert running like a flat carpet to the terrible mountain ranges of the Kunluns and the Karakaroms. Thermal socks, dried fruit, chocolate . . . the supposition she had drawn still shocked her.

But as she slipped into her robe and headed for bed she knew there was still another, even more shocking suspicion that she had consigned to the periphery of her thoughts, not allowing it entry, stubbornly resisting it because if she

brought it out and looked at it, she would understand
Bishop's fears for her. Turning out the lights she once
again refused it entry and succeeded in pushing it far
enough away to fall asleep at once.

4

IN THE MORNING IRIS MADE HER APPEARANCE IN JEANS, and after faithfully escorting her downstairs Mrs. Pollifax could see that emotional support would no longer be needed: Jenny whistled, Malcolm gave her a second calm glance, and George Westrum's eyes rested on her with a glow that Mrs. Pollifax hoped Iris noticed, but doubted that she did; Joe Forbes murmured, "Well, now," and even Peter Fox looked mildly appreciative. It was true that at breakfast Iris tipped a plate of peanuts into her lap, with half of them cascading to the floor, but—as Jenny cheerfully pointed out—peanuts were easier to recover than spilled beer. Iris, thought Mrs. Pollifax, was in danger of being assigned the role of comic in the group.

At breakfast and again at lunch Mrs. Pollifax pursued

her responsibility of listing for Mr. Li what each person particularly wanted to see, and in this she found no surprises: Joe Forbes wanted to visit a university, Jenny the second-grade class in a school, and George listed only communes. Malcolm's priorities were more numerous and entirely cultural. Young Peter repeated his request for a side trip to the village where his grandmother was born, while Iris wanted to see the Chinese Opera but especially the Ban Po Village Museum in Xian because the artifacts reflected a Neolithic society run by women eight thousand years ago. Women's Lib again. For herself, Mrs. Pollifax wrote down the Drum Tower in Xian and hoped no one would ask why. After consulting her guidebook she added the Bell Tower for camouflage, and any Buddhist temples.

But Guangzhou, or Canton, she found, was mainly a waiting game. She enjoyed their trip to the bank to exchange travelers' checks for tourist scrip: she watched in fascination as four clerks hovered over her money, carefully checking the amount on an abacus. But tourist money, Mr. Li told them, could not be spent on the streets, at the bazaars, or free markets, only in the government-run shops.

Mrs. Pollifax at once rose to this challenge. "How can I get real money?" she asked him, thinking ahead to possible exigencies, and was told that the Friendship Stores would no doubt give real Chinese currency in change, whereupon she promptly asked for large denominations of tourist scrip, determined to collect as many of the authentic bills as she could. "My new hobby," she told Malcolm cheerfully.

Aside from this, the Dr. Sun Yet-sen Memorial charmed her with its gorgeously intense blue-laquered tiles, but it smelled musty inside; she obediently oh-d and ah-d at the pandas in the zoo, but the heat there at midday nearly felled her, and once again they lunched on the second floor of a restaurant, with the natives on the street floor below.

Only once was she fully startled out of her lingering

jet-lag apathy. With an unexpected half hour of time confronting Mr. Tung, he offered them a pleasant stroll down a suburban road that held a mixture of older buildings among the brand-new scaffold-laced structures. One building in particular caught Mrs. Pollifax's eye, creamy-white against the dull cement facade of its neighbors, and of an architecture that she could only identify in her mind as tropical-colonial. Graceful arched windows, each one trimmed in a tender green, were set like jewels into the smooth creamy walls. Next to an open green door hung a vertical sign, and Mrs. Pollifax brought out her small camera and took a picture of the charming vignette: a courtyard, a door, a leafy green tree, a donkey cart parked next to the door.

"What does the sign say?" she called to Mr. Tung, pointing.

Moving to her side he looked at it. "People's Security Bureau," he said, and abruptly turned away, his face expressionless.

People's Security Bureau . . . the Sepos, she remembered from her reading, and she wondered if, since Mao's death, the Sepos still knocked on doors at midnight to take people away, or whether the new order had changed this. She hoped so. Bishop had said, "You'll find many surprising changes happening there, but they've been taking place very cautiously, very slowly." She lingered a moment gazing at the open door, trying to imagine what lay behind its innocent facade, and then she turned and hurried away, made uneasy by a vague sense of foreboding.

"What did he say that building was?" asked George Westrum, catching up with her.

"People's Security Bureau."

"Oh, cops. By the way, did you know Malcolm writes kiddies' books?"

The tone of his voice, she thought, would not have

surprised Malcolm. "Yes, very fine ones," she told him. "Perhaps your children—are you married, George?"

He shook his head. "Never had children, been a widower for years. Tell me why in hell a man would write children's books? Hasn't he grown up yet?"

Mrs. Pollifax glanced at George's baseball cap, tilted boyishly at the back of his head, and smiled. "Do any of us?" she asked dryly. "And should we—completely?"

He didn't hear her; he said abruptly, "There's Iris Damson up ahead. Doesn't realize it's almost time to be heading for the bus. Excuse me, I'll just hurry along and tell her."

She watched him march briskly toward Iris, passing Joe Forbes photographing workers mixing cement, then Peter and Jenny taking pictures of each other, and Malcolm aiming his camera at children playing. She smiled, thinking George Westrum was showing very definite signs of becoming addicted to Iris.

In late afternoon they reached the airport, where they said good-bye to Mr. Tung. Because there were no reserved seats on the plane, not even for foreigners, there was a mad dash across the tarmac once the plane was announced, and the group found themselves widely dispersed throughout the small two-engine prop plane. Mrs. Pollifax settled herself into an aisle seat with two men in Mao jackets beside her, and realized, now that she had sampled a little of China, it was time she began considering just how she was going to approach Comrade Guo Musu in his barbershop near the Drum Tower in Xian. She found that no inspiration occurred to her at all; she had no idea what the Drum Tower might be, and not even her wildest flights of imagination could conjure up the appearance of a barbershop, which in China would scarcely announce itself with a striped barber pole. It troubled her, too, that so far the tour appeared to be arranged to prevent even the most accidental of encounters with the Chinese, and up against these frustrations she began to reflect instead on just which member of the group might be her coagent. One of them—*one person on this plane*—knew what Xian meant, and why she was here.

One person, she reflected, and again asked, who? Which one?

From where he sat on the plane he could just see the back of Mrs. Pollifax's head several seats down the aisle, and as the plane lifted he wondered what she was thinking about as they took flight to Xian, and to Guo Musu, and he wondered how in hell she was going to extract information from a total stranger, given so little time and the watchful eye of Mr. Li. Once again he shook his head over Carstairs' choice; they had a very tight schedule, and if she failed in this contact it was highly doubtful that he would ever find the labor camp by himself. The distances were too vast, and their time too painfully limited.

He had programmed himself not to think ahead, but separated from the others now, with two native Chinese between him and the window, he allowed his mind to wander a little from the discipline he'd imposed upon it. He already knew how tough his assignment was going to be, and how the rescue of X—if it could be accomplished—was only the beginning of it. It brought a curious feeling to know so much intellectually about China and to apply this knowledge on arrival to the country's reality: it felt positively schizophrenic, for instance, to be listening with half his mind to the conversation between the two Chinese next to him, to understand every word they said yet pretend that he didn't.

In Guangzhou he'd been sorely tempted to buy a newspaper, a copy of *Zhong Guo Qing Nian Bao*—the

China Youth Daily—which he was accustomed to reading weeks late, in America. This he had resisted, allowing himself only a glance at its headlines. The two men on his right were discussing production figures. They were both foremen in a factory returning home to Xian after a meeting of cadres in Guangzhou. He was curious about them. They were in their fifties; one had mentioned that he was born in Nanjing, while the other came from a village outside Beijing.

To live now in Xian, so far away, he thought, it would have been *shang-shan-xia-xiang* that wrenched them from their native towns and families, or what was called "up to the mountains and down to the villages," that great experiment of Mao's that sent intellectuals into the country to dig wells and plow fields, and peasants out of the villages to be trained and educated. He understood the need; there were too many people in China's cities, and it was vital to spread them out, except that usually only the peasants— the *jie ho*—were ever returned to their native villages. The educated young people, the *chi-shi qingnian*—found themselves banished forever to the countryside. He wondered how *he* would feel if, upon graduating from college, he were to be sent off to a remote Inner Mongolian commune, for instance, to be *tu bao zi,* a hick—literally a clod of earth—for the rest of his life. It had been one of the most astonishing leveling experiments in modern history, the attempt to reeducate nearly a billion people in the "correct" ideological way to think, as against an incorrect way . . . the turning over of one's heart and mind to the Motherland, the achievement of absolute trust in the parent-state. *Work without laying down conditions. Work without expecting reward. It is the work that counts, not the person. What helps our reform we should talk about abundantly, what is bad for reform we should not talk about at all. Education Through Labor. Dui shi, bi dui ren—it is the mistake we are after, not the man. Be grateful to the state by working with enthusiasm, without thinking of yourself.*

Except that for X it was not education through labor, but reform through labor, and what would Wang be like after his years in a reform camp? To survive he would have learned humility through self-criticism and confession; he would have been taught over and over that he must selflessly work for the greater whole, because whatever changes had occurred since Mao's death it was doubtful that they would easily reach a labor camp in a remote province. If by now Wang had not turned into a model prisoner, thinking "correct" ideological thoughts, he could just as easily have given up hope and have become a shell of a man. Would he even consent to leave, to escape?

Would he even find Wang? And if he found the camp, would he be able to recognize him? What if he had been altered beyond recognition? From some ancient file there had arrived that single blown-up photograph of a younger Wang . . . *Comrade Wang, engineer, greeting volunteer workers for our Motherland's defenses as they arrive in the north from villages and cities all over our country to joyously give of their labor.* There had been no date on the photo, just as there was no knowing what political tide had swept him aside, condemned of revisionist thinking or of being an anti-revolutionist.

There were the other unknowns and variables as well: the fact that the only information they had about the logging camp was its existence somewhere in the Tian Shan mountain range and surrounded on three sides by a stream of water so fast-flowing that it couldn't be crossed except on horseback. Not that the poor devils needed such barriers, he reflected, because if a prisoner decided to escape, where could he go? He needed identity papers, authorization for travel, and coupons for food and clothing, and wherever he went he would still be in China.

Such thoughts as these didn't undermine his confidence, they were merely parts of a logistics problem that would have to be solved as they left Xian and drew closer to Urumchi and to the Tian Shan range. He knew that he was well trained, that he was nerveless and capable, and he spoke the language fluently. The most aggravating unknown was Mrs. Pollifax. He objected very much to having the success of his assignment rest just now in someone else's hands, much less those of a foolish middle-aged lady. He had fought against this from the beginning, insisting he manage the contact himself, but Carstairs had said, "We can't risk you, the contact in Xian is too pivotal, too dangerous. If you should be caught—if Guo should betray you—we'd lose you, and you're irreplaceable because of your background in the country. The situation needs someone entirely different, someone so outwardly innocent that she'll deflect suspicion."

"She?" he'd repeated sharply.

And Carstairs had smiled pleasantly and said, "Yes, we have a woman in mind."

So here they were, the two of them, locked together into this situation for better or for worse, flying over mountains the color and shape of camels' humps, in a country whose culture was among the most ancient in the world. And he loved this country, which was a strange thing to discover because he loved so few things. Because of this he knew that he hated Mao for setting China back decades with his cultural revolution that wiped out intellectuals, closed universities, nearly destroyed art and science, and, in turn, brought only a new form of corruption out of the corruptions he'd intended to erase. Well, that was long since over; both Mao and the more liberal Chou were dead, and new leaders in command, but the country was still filled with Maoists. He thought wryly of the current political metaphor, "the two ends are hot and the middle is cold," a very Chinese way of saying that change was passionately wanted at both the top and the bottom of the society, but sitting squarely in the middle in many areas were Mao's bureaucrats, threatened by the progressive changes, indignant, clinging in fury to the old status quo. The reformers were listening, though: how could they help but hear the people at the Democracy Wall in 1979? The people still waited with infinite patience for the democracy that had been promised them once by Mao.

He turned and looked at the two men beside him, wishing he might ask them a thousand questions. Seeing him glance toward them they smiled, eager to show their friendship.

"Ni hao," he said, carefully avoiding any tonal pronunciation, rendering the greeting flat and drawling and clumsy.

The man next to him nodded vigorously; the second man by the window leaned forward to give him an eager smile and a thumbs-up gesture, and he was offered a Double Happiness brand cigarette, which he politely refused. As they returned to their conversation he glanced down the aisle and saw Mrs. Pollifax and her two seat companions stand up and change places with an extravagant exchange of bows and smiles: she was being given the window seat, and he wondered wryly how she had accomplished this without language.

He wondered, too, how much she guessed when she had been told so little.

He wondered if it had occurred to her yet that if Mr. Wang's rescue was a success, the man was going to have to be accompanied out of China—escorted, led, or dragged out, depending on his sympathies and his state of mind.

He wondered if she realized that in order to accompany Wang out of the country he himself was going to have to disappear from the tour group—and foreigners were simply not allowed to disappear into China. When would she recognize the fact that the whole purpose of the tour was to allow him to vanish—and that indeed all of them were hostages to his success in disappearing . . .

It was a woman guide who met them at the airport in Xian, and Mrs. Pollifax was amused by the look of awe and delight on Iris' face at sight of her. Apparently Mr. Li knew the woman from previous trips and greeted her cordially. "This is Miss Bai," he told them, introducing her.

She was a slightly built woman, older than Mr. Li, very serious and intense, in fact one could guess her efficiency by the way that Mr. Li subtly relaxed on finding her there. Noticing this Mrs. Pollifax experienced a sudden insight into the tensions behind Mr. Li's nervous laugh: the necessity to please not only the people he guided but also nameless faceless superiors who had selected him out of thousands to associate with foreigners.

"You will not be far out of town here," he told them cheerfully. "The hotel is in the middle of Xian."

"Horray," cried Jenny.

Because they had all been separated on the plane Mrs. Pollifax noticed that they met now like long-lost friends. Even Peter looked less sullen, and as they headed for their next minibus she heard him asking Malcolm about his books—word had spread quickly, she thought dryly—while Joe Forbes was teasing Jenny about her hair, which she'd braided into a pigtail. "Going native, huh?" he said, pointing to a girl on the street with a similar thick braid down her back.

"I can't wait to buy a Mao jacket and cap," she told him. "Wait till you see me then!"

"You wish such purchases?" asked Miss Bai, overhearing her. "I will arrange for a visit to a department store tomorrow."

"Wonderful," breathed Jenny. "Thanks!"

Xian was the color of the mountains they'd flown over, terra-cotta and dusty, with patches of green only in the long lines of newly planted poplar trees and in an occasional rice field. New cement apartment houses were being built, but they were windowless and unfinished, still outnumbered by the old walled compounds along the road and the tiny mud-and-straw homes glimpsed behind them. Their bus drove toward the city through pedestrians and bicyclists, constantly sounding its horn. Entering Xian the landscape changed, the buildings drew closer together, they met with billboards lining each intersection where once Mao's thoughts must have been inscribed but which now advertised soap and toilet paper and toothpaste.

This time their hotel sat squarely in the center of town on a busy street. In Canton there had been lingering traces of the European influence, but here the architecture was Russian, a massive square hotel built of gray cement with a wall and a sentry at the gate. The Chinese spirit had asserted itself, however, with a huge scarlet sign on which gold letters in Chinese and English proclaimed THE THEORETICAL BASIS GUIDING OUR THINKING IS MARXISM AND LENINISM. MAO TSE-TUNG.

Iris regarded this in despair. "I've not *read* Marx," she cried. "What was his approach to women?"

"Cautious," said Malcolm.

"I'll bet yours is, too," Jenny told him.

"Naturally," he said, "or I'd not be a bachelor."

"Are you really!" Jenny exclaimed happily. "Not even one very *little* marriage somewhere?"

Mrs. Pollifax gave Jenny a sharp glance. On the surface she thought Jenny insouciant and lively, yet she'd begun to notice a strange bite to her words. It was present when she mocked Iris' clumsiness, and it was in the tone of her voice now, a curious recklessness, a sense of trying too hard. *There is a suggestion of desperation here,* she thought, and wondered why.

Mr. Li interrupted her speculations with an announcement. Dinner, he said, would be served in twenty minutes, and he pointed to the building where it would be served, and for the evening, if they wished, they could stroll to the People's Park together while he and Miss Bai worked out their schedule for Xian. Next he explained that there were no keys to the rooms at the People's Hotel—there was no need for keys—and he read out their room numbers.

"I don't like there being no keys," Jenny complained as they climbed the stairs to the floor above.

"I think," said Mrs. Pollifax, "one has to bear in mind that the hotel is run by the government, and there's a soldier on duty at the entrance, and as you can see," she added as they reached the second floor, "there's a chap at a desk to check people."

"But there are so many workers here," Jenny protested.

Malcolm fielded that one. "Plum job, my dear. If it even occurred to one of them to steal something—doubtful— where would they sell it? Don't be so suspicious," he chided, adding dryly, "this isn't America, you know. Who's for that stroll after dinner, by the way?"

After one look at her room Mrs. Pollifax decided very firmly to opt for the walk to People's Park. She could not conceive of an evening spent in a room so small, so unbelievably dark and hot, with a tiny air-conditioner that made chuckling sounds when she turned it on. She therefore set out with the others following dinner, and falling into step beside Iris she asked how things were going.

Iris did not fail her. "Oh isn't it *wonderful?*" she cried, turning to face Mrs. Pollifax and very nearly falling over a stone in her path. "I asked Miss Bai what her first name is. I have it written down somewhere, but in English it means Elder Fragrance, isn't that beautiful?"

"Really lovely, yes," agreed Mrs. Pollifax, "but I think you'd better watch out for the holes in this sidewalk, Iris."

"Okay. But what's with this Peter Fox?" she asked. "I sat next to him at dinner and I don't know when I've met anyone so grumpy—unless it was Stanley before he had his morning coffee. Is he going to be a real wet blanket?"

"He may thaw, given time," said Mrs. Pollifax generously. "It seems his grandmother gave him this trip as a present because she was born in China and can't come herself. I daresay he'd much rather be off backpacking somewhere with a group of friends."

"If he has any friends," said Iris. "Well, I can see how he feels, of course, but if somebody gave me a present—any kind of present—you wouldn't catch me sulking like that. And a free trip to China—wow!"

Mrs. Pollifax smiled faintly, noting the words *if anyone gave me a present, any kind of present,* and reflected that Iris would be too busy giving presents to receive any; the takers must flock to her like bees to a honey flower. A pity, she thought, and said mischievously, "George Westrum seems very nice."

Iris warmly agreed. "Oh, isn't he? And I think"—she lowered her voice—"I think he used to be an FBI man, isn't that intriguing?"

"FBI?" repeated Mrs. Pollifax alertly. "How very exciting!"

Iris nodded. "Now all we need is someone from the CIA."

"Yes indeed," murmured Mrs. Pollifax, without so much as a blink of an eye. "Quite horrid people, I'm sure."

"Oh there must be *some* nice people among them," Iris conceded with her radiant smile and then, glancing ahead,

"Look—that must be the park. We're here! Except why are the others huddling around the gate?"

"Because it costs money," shouted Malcolm, as Iris called out her query, crossing the avenue. "The real stuff. Either of you have any?"

"I have," Iris announced, joining them. "I bought those white jade cups at Canton airport, remember?" As the natives gathered to watch, she dug into her purse, brought out small wrinkled bills and then several coins and presented them to the man. He selected several *fen*, beamed at her, and issued them tickets.

"Now this," said Joe Forbes as they entered, "has to be the real China."

Mrs. Pollifax was inclined to believe him. There were paths to the right and to the left, but she was drawn instead toward a crowd straight ahead from which, even at a distance, she could hear roars of laughter. Joining it Mrs. Pollifax stood on tiptoe to peer over heads and found them gathered around a television set, a modest and perfectly normal television set plugged into some unseen outlet in the out-of-doors, with cartoons dancing across its screen. Amazing she thought, and looked instead into the faces of the people watching the cartoons, touched by their innocent excitement and joy.

The subtitles, however, were in Chinese, and presently—still smiling at the pleasure it was giving—she moved away to investigate a small growing crowd off to the left, and discovered Malcolm seated under a tree sketching. Not far away George Westrum was attempting sign language with a young woman, with Joe Forbes chuckling at his elbow. At once a young man spotted Mrs. Pollifax and hurried to her side. "You are American too," he cried eagerly. "I may ask questions?"

"Oh yes," she told him warmly. "*Ni hao!* Good evening!"

His boldness, his daring, immediately drew people from Malcolm's circle into his, and Mrs. Pollifax found herself smiled at and approved as the audience waited with attention for their comrade to address this visitor from a country halfway across the world. Their pride in him was palpable, and Mrs. Pollifax waited too, her heart beating a trifle faster at the importance of this moment.

"In America," he said slowly, his brows knitted together by the seriousness with which he, too, regarded this moment, "you grow cotton?"

Mrs. Pollifax, a little surprised, nodded her head. "Yes. Oh yes. In our southern states."

"Suzzen states?"

"Warm places," she explained. "Like Canton?"

"Canton?" He looked bewildered, and she saw that they had suddenly lost their way; the eagerness still hung between them, tangible but severely threatened.

"No," she said, trying to retrieve direction, "in the United States, where I live. Where——" She was suddenly overwhelmed by the nouns, pronouns, verbs that separated them and with which she must frame a sentence, acutely aware too of the perplexities of *for* and *about* and *from;* the wall between them seemed opaque, the gulf immeasurable, and then with sudden inspiration she remembered the snapshots she had crammed into her purse at the last minute. She reached into her purse and drew them out: a photograph of her apartment house, with herself standing in front of it; several of her grandson opening packages at Christmas in her living room; one of Cyrus, and two of her geraniums. She offered them to this new friend. With great wonder her pictures were accepted, people crowded in to peer over his shoulder, they were then distributed by the young man, one by one, moving from hand to hand accompanied by murmurs of awe and surprise.

"*Snow?*" asked her friend, pointing to the picture of her standing in front of her apartment house.

"Yes," she said, nodding happily. "Yes, snow. Too cold there for *cotton*."

"Ah—I see, I see," he cried in relief, understanding, and addressed his friends rapidly and with authority.

"Husband?" he asked, pointing to Cyrus.

She smiled. "A *very* dear friend."

"Aha," he cried joyously, and again addressed the crowd, but it was the photographs of her grandson that drew the most appreciative murmurs, and she was given glances of deep respect.

A picture, she thought, *was certainly worth a thousand words; hadn't it been the Chinese who first said this?*

Her friend was thanking her now with pleasure. "Now we see, yes," he said. He turned and spoke sharply to one of the men holding a picture and snatched it back, rubbing away a smudge of dirt before he returned it to her. One by one the snapshots arrived in her hands and she put them away. It seemed an auspicious moment to withdraw. "I go now," she told them all, bowing. "Good night and thank you! *Zai jian!*"

"*Good* day," they called, laughing with her, and as she left they surged again toward Malcolm and his sketchbook.

Mrs. Pollifax wandered on along the path, ignoring a charming arched bridge over a pond and drawn toward a mysterious bright light in the distance. Iris, catching up with her, said, "I'm ready to go back, it's growing dark."

"Hi there," called Jenny, emerging from a side path. "Going back?"

"Yes," said Mrs. Pollifax, "but not until I've investigated that bright light ahead. I'm curious—I noticed it when we entered the park and it's still there."

"Noises, too," contributed Iris as they strolled toward it.

"Of people?" asked Jenny doubtfully.

"Weird sounds," Iris decided. "People and engines. An adventure for us maybe?"

"Definitely," said Mrs. Pollifax happily. "Let's look and find out."

Out of the darkness, the light emerging from its interior, appeared a circular wooden structure with steps leading to the top and the silhouette of heads lining a platform that encircled the structure. "Yes, yes," said the solitary attendant leaning against a step, and untied a rope to allow them free entry. They mounted narrow precipitous wooden stairs—up, up, toward the suffused brilliant light—to find themselves peering down into an arena with gently sloping sides.

"Good heavens," breathed Iris, "it's like looking into a barrel, it's so small. Look—two motorcycles!"

As they watched, two splendidly dressed young men emerged from a small door and mounted the cycles, the crowd murmured appreciatively, the young men bowed, grinned, rev'd up the engines to a roar, rode once around the floor, and then as they gained speed they sent their cycles upward and into the curve of the wall. Mrs. Pollifax braced herself as the cyclists circled higher and higher, engines roaring, the platform creaking and trembling and shuddering under her feet. The cyclists became perpendicular now, and for one moment she thought they might shoot out over the top, taking people and platform with them (headline: *Xian, People's Republic: In China today dozens were killed when two performing cyclists went out of control and careened into the audience. Among the dead, three American tourists, as yet unidentified.*), and then the engines slackened, the momentum was aborted and—perhaps most difficult of all—the two shining young gods guided their vehicles down, still spinning off the walls, reached bottom, and came to an earth-trembling stop. Off came the helmets; the cheers were thunderous and joyful.

Mrs. Pollifax joined the applause; it was over, they had arrived at the end. Slowly they descended the steps with the crowd, to the hard-packed earth where a single light now illuminated the path. "Now *that*," she said, "was slightly incredible."

"So was that platform," commented Jenny. "It felt like an upside-down bushel basket and just as frail. I was scared to death."

"Never mind, it was fun," breathed Iris, her eyes shining.

Already the lights were being extinguished all over the park; nothing was wasted, it was nine o'clock, the television screen was dark, the park emptying. They walked out onto the avenue where the small garish lamps of the vendors shone like fireflies in the darkness. People lingered, chatting, under the dim light of the occasional streetlamp, some strolling in pairs, some hurrying home, a few on bicycles.

"Now which way did we come?" asked Iris.

"Oh—down that road," Mrs. Pollifax said, pointing.

Jenny shook her head. "Uh-huh, that's where we saw George taking pictures, don't you remember? So we take the other street."

Mrs. Pollifax expressed her doubt. "I really don't think so."

"But I'm *known* for my bump of direction," Jenny insisted. "Really I am . . . trust me!"

"We'll trust you," Iris told her gravely.

They reached, eventually, the broad avenue on which they had expected to find the People's Hotel, but there was no hotel. Instead they met with a sea of people strolling down the center of a road in a silence broken only by the shuffling sounds of their feet. There were no cars. As they continued walking there was no hotel, either. They were looked at with curiosity; a few turned to stare.

"Still confident?" Mrs. Pollifax asked Jenny.

"Oh yes," said Jenny, and then spoiled such assertiveness by pausing to say to a young man, "Do you speak English?"

He smiled, shook his head, and hurried on. So did they, but after three more blocks Mrs. Pollifax's skepticism had turned into alarm; she decided the time had come to try that universal language of the hands. She stopped two men, and laid her head on her hands in a manner that she hoped denoted sleep. "Ho-tel?" she asked. "Hotel?"

The two men nodded happily and turned to point in the direction ahead of them.

"Xiexie," she said, bowing.

But another block still produced no hotel, and Mrs. Pollifax began to picture them sleeping in a doorway for the night, began to look down narrow alleys and into mysterious entrances that led to wooden doors, speculating on how long a tourist might be lost in Xian, and longing passionately for a real bed.

It was Iris who next said, "I don't see a damn thing ahead resembling a hotel. Let me try."

"But I'm supposed to have such a good bump of direction," wailed Jenny.

"Well, coming to China has dislocated it, I think," said Mrs. Pollifax.

"Ho-tel?" asked Iris, stopping three men and repeating Mrs. Pollifax's symbol for sleep.

At once Iris drew a crowd; they became surrounded by faces made dim and unearthly in the near-darkness, faces marveling at Iris' height, a few women tittering behind their hands; it turned into a party, and a few minutes later a dozen of the young men escorted them half a block farther, smiling and murmuring "ho-tel" and pointing, and there—at last—was the hotel, with its sentry and its gate.

Bows, thank yous, and smiles were exchanged, they passed through a deserted lobby, mounted stairs, and Mrs. Pollifax entered her small hot room with its chuckling air-conditioner. The temperature had dropped only a few degrees and she found the twenty-five-watt light in the lamp depressing. Kneeling beside her suitcase she unlocked and opened it to return the camera she'd extracted from it before walking to the park, and suddenly became very still, the movement of camera to suitcase arrested.

Her suitcase had been opened and searched while she was gone.

A long time ago she had worked out a formula for packing, and although efficiency had been only a minor reason for this she had automatically continued to pack in a certain way even when there was no necessity for caution. She had felt there was no need for caution on this trip, but apparently she had been wrong. Her suitcase had been unlocked very expertly, and very professionally and discreetly searched, but whoever had done the job couldn't possibly have known of her packing formula. When she had snatched the camera from her suitcase after dinner her bright red pajamas had as usual been folded up with the pajama bottoms underneath the pajama tops—that was the important detail—and her toothbrush and comb tucked into their folds. Now the pajama bottoms were on top, and both toothbrush and comb had vanished somewhere into her suitcase.

Now this, thought Mrs. Pollifax, abruptly sitting down on the floor, *is a pretty kettle of fish, and completely unexpected.*

Who, she wondered, *could have done this?* She could not believe it had been a worker in the hotel; opening a locked suitcase without leaving behind so much as a scratch was an art denied to the average person.

The police? But Mr. Li had handled Customs, and at the border no one had felt any need to question her about her remarkable supply of vitamins and dried fruit.

Her mysterious coagent? But whoever he was there seemed no need for him to investigate her; he had the advantage of knowing who she was, as well as what she'd brought with her.

What a bewildering finish to a delightful evening, she thought, and realized that she felt thoroughly jarred by this. *I don't understand it*, she reflected, *and I don't like it, It's almost as if—* But she did not allow herself to complete that thought, and hastily drew out her pajamas.

5

"MAY WE SEE THE SKETCHES YOU DID LAST EVENING IN the park?" Mrs. Pollifax asked Malcolm at breakfast.

He said ruefully, "I ended up giving them all away to my audience. We certainly attract crowds, don't we?"

He smiled across the table at Iris, who flushed as usual but managed one of her radiant smiles in return.

"Quite a schedule today," commented Joe Forbes, spearing a peanut between his chopsticks.

"Yes indeed," she said. Miss Bai had pinned to the dining room wall a calendar of events for their stay in Xian, presented in flawless calligraphy, but to Mrs. Pollifax the most important news was that after trips to the Bell Tower and to the Wild Goose Pagoda, they were going to visit the Drum Tower.

For the Drum Tower Mrs. Pollifax still had no plans. How very easy and natural the assignment had seemed to her when she was sitting in Carstairs' office in Langley Field, Virginia, and how very different it looked now that she was in Xian! She had absolutely no idea what obstacles were going to greet her, or even whether she would be able to find Guo Musu's barbershop. She dared not ask about a barbershop near the Drum Tower or she would be shown it—if it existed—in the company of Mr. Li or Miss Bai. She had finally accepted the fact that she could assemble no strategy whatever in advance, which was not the happiest way to approach such an important moment, or the Drum Tower either, or Guo Musu if he could be found, but Mrs. Pollifax had a great deal of faith: something would occur to her. A miracle would take place.

Yes, definitely a miracle, she told herself firmly.

In the meantime they were going to visit Ban Po Village this morning, which would please Iris, and a department store, which would please Jenny's desire for Mao cap and jacket, and Mrs. Pollifax tried to pretend that it pleased her too, that this was a perfectly normal day with the afternoon of no particular significance, and that her suitcase had not been searched the night before.

At Ban Po Village they were ushered into a briefing room and seated at a long table with a tea cup placed squarely in front of each chair, and while they sipped hot tea the resident guide delivered facts to them, translated into English by Miss Bai . . . the site discovered accidentally in 1953 . . . the foundations of forty-five houses with remarkably preserved pottery and tools . . . in existence from 6080 B.C. to 5600 B.C. . . . evidence of its being a matriarchal society . . .

Released from the tyranny of the briefing, Mrs. Pollifax considered those facts. She decided that facts could not possibly describe the drama of workmen starting to build a factory here and discovering instead the remains of an eight-thousand-year-old village. Strolling along the walkways of the building that sheltered the excavation, she tried to come to grips with eight thousand years of time and failed. Eight thousand was only a number, there was simply no way to cope with such aeons, but what did come to her—like a lingering fragrance across the years—was the intelligence at work here: the intricately worked out trenches between the houses, the playful designs etched into pottery, the burial of dead children in huge egg-shaped pottery urns, as if to return them, she thought, to the embryo from which they'd entered life. It gave her a pleasant feeling of pride in the human race. She wondered what archaeologists in the year A.D. 10,000 would find when they uncovered the relics of the twentieth century; would there, she wondered, be any signs of intelligence remaining? or only vestiges of folly and violence?

On the drive back to Xian she began to feel oppressively hungry. Miss Bai was explaining to Peter and Jenny the government's current Five Stresses—civilization, morality, order, cleanliness, and manners, and the Four Beautifications —of thought, language, heart, and environment—and Mrs. Pollifax was ashamed of herself for yawning. "Why do I get hungry so early?" she complained to Joe Forbes, sitting next to her.

"Peanuts for breakfast?" he quipped amiably.

"But I also had a hard-boiled egg," she protested.

Malcolm called across the aisle, "I'd say it's the chopsticks. You may *think* you eat a lot—"

Iris turned around in the seat ahead and said, "But she's the most expert of us all, haven't you noticed?" She beamed at Mrs. Pollifax. "Wasn't Ban Po Village tremendous? I hope I didn't monopolize the guide, but honestly— eight thousand years! I mean the Qin Shi Huang Tombs we see tomorrow are only 210 B.C."

"Practically contemporary," put in Malcolm mischievously. "Possibly it's culture that's giving us an appetite?"

But Mrs. Pollifax's eyes were on George Westrum who was seated next to Iris, and who had turned now to give Iris a glance that startled Mrs. Pollifax. She thought: *George is on his way to adoring this woman . . .* It was a peculiar word to choose but it was the word that had slid into her head: *adoration,* she mused. *Devotion. Worship.*

The alliances that were beginning to form had already begun to interest her. The infants, for instance—as Malcolm continued to call Peter and Jenny—had at once formed a twosome. Iris talked to everyone, but Mrs. Pollifax noticed how often George Westrum managed to sit next to her, his face inscrutable, his eyes watching every play of expression across her vivid face. When Malcolm joined them George's eyes shifted to Malcolm's face, again without expression. Iris appeared to regard Malcolm with some caution and blushed a great deal, but Mrs. Pollifax wasn't sure whether it was his charm or his book writing that dazzled her.

As for Joe Forbes, Mrs. Pollifax admitted that she'd not yet fathomed him at all. He was always with them—smiling and amiable—and often contributing a brief comment or wisecrack, but he was oddly *not* there somehow. She wondered if anyone else had noticed this. Not consciously, she decided, but his personality had so little impact that once or twice she'd caught someone adding, "Oh yes, and Joe too."

She wondered if this meant that he was the agent who would eventually approach her after her attempt this afternoon at the Drum Tower. Her knowledge of professional agents was limited and theatrical, but she had heard that certain full-time agents took great pains to rub out their personalities and achieve anonymity; perhaps this became habitual, and the loss of personality irreversible. *Except, of course, for John Sebastian Farrell*, she thought with a smile, *who only heaped new layers of personality on his own to gloriously and cheekily distract.*

She was still smiling, still thinking of Farrell, when they drew up to the department store in Xian.

"A *real* department store?" asked Jenny skeptically.

Mr. Li assured her that yes this was a real one, where the Chinese people shopped. "But they will also take your tourist script here, and you have forty minutes to look."

"Forty minutes!" wailed Jenny. "To find a Mao cap and jacket? Peter wants to buy them, too. Oh yes, and Joe," she added.

"Miss Bai—?"

Miss Bai nodded. "I'll go with them."

"Anyone else?"

No one else had any pressing needs. They entered the store together to immediately veer off in different directions. The first floor was high-ceilinged and large and struck Mrs. Pollifax as curiously empty, which was puzzling to her because throngs of people lined the counters. She realized she was associating it with American department stores, which were all color, movement, and glamorous displays, and at once felt penitent. Turning right she began a tour of the broad and dusty aisles, hungering for color to relieve the dull greens and grays and blues, and was suddenly brought to a standstill by a wall that blazed with color.

"Books," she whispered in delight: books placed side by side against the wall so that their jackets bloomed like flowers. She moved toward them, and the people crowding around the counter made room for her. *"Xiexie,"* she said quietly, taking her place.

But she was a foreigner, after all, and the clerk hurried to her, smiling. Mrs. Pollifax thought, *I'll buy one, I'll buy a book as my souvenir here.* She pointed to a paperback with a jacket design that stood out from the others because it did not have an illustration of a soldier, or a girl and a boy. "That one," she said, drawn by its black and white lines splashed with abstract yellows and scarlets.

The girl's hands hovered, then dropped. She picked out a cream-colored book next to Mrs. Pollifax's choice and placed it in her hands.

"No," said Mrs. Pollifax politely. "No, not this one," She shook her head and then glanced down at the book and opened it to see what it was. She found maps inside: it was a purse-sized atlas of China, the cities and towns marked in Chinese with not a single English word to be seen, and therefore incomprehensible and useless to her. On the other hand, she mused, it could make a lovely souvenir for her grandson, who would be pleased and amused by it. "I'll take it," she said, nodding, "but I'd also like—" and she pointed again to the charming cover that had originally caught her eye. Several more books were picked up and put down before the one she wanted was achieved. It turned out to be a recipe book, also in Chinese, but with lavish color photos at the back.

"I'll take both," she said, holding up two fingers and smiling. Reaching for her purse the crowd drew closer while she and the salesgirl sorted through her Chinese currency for the *yuan* that would purchase one recipe book and one book of maps.

And then—suddenly jarred—she thought, *"Maps?"*

Maps, she repeated, the word tugging at her mind, and she picked up the atlas and looked again at its competently waterproof cream jacket. This time she opened it more thoughtfully. On page one she found a map of the entire country, with each province in a different color. She could recognize the Xinjiang Autonomous Region because of its size—enormous—and its location in the northwest corner.

After studying the shape of it she turned the pages until she found the identical shape on page thirty-eight.

Which means, she thought in amazement, *that I'm actually staring at a map of Xinjiang Province with all its roads laid out in front of me and marked, and all its towns and villages identified, even if their names are written in Chinese, which I can't read.*

But Guo Musu—if she found him—could read them.

And standing there in the middle of China, in a department store in Shaanxi Province surrounded by eavesdroppers and interested spectators, Mrs. Pollifax began to laugh. Her laugh began as a chuckle that traveled up from her toes and emerged as a luxurious, Cheshire-cat smile that lighted up her face.

Her miracle had just happened.

"I'll buy two of these," she told the clerk, holding up the atlas, and reached into her purse for another *yuan.*

To the others, back in the bus, she showed only her recipe book. Peter, Jenny, and Joe Forbes were happily wearing their new Mao caps and jackets ("show and tell time," laughed Jenny); Iris had bought a bright enameled mug, Malcolm an ink stick, and George a handkerchief with Xian printed on it.

"A taste of the consumer life," commented Malcolm dryly, "to keep us from suffering withdrawal pangs."

They lunched. They visited a cloisonné factory where they had a long tea-and-briefing, due mainly to Iris asking far too many questions about workers' hours and wages; they were led through dark and dusty halls to watch cloisonné jewelry intricately crafted, and then to a Friendship Store for purchases. They visited the Bell Tower, and the Wild Goose Pagoda, except that by midafternoon it was so hot that only Jenny and Peter climbed the eight stories to its peak.

And then in late afternoon they came to the Drum Tower, and Mrs. Pollifax's moment of truth had arrived.

6

Mrs. Pollifax descended last of all from the minibus, trying not to remember that she'd flown halfway around the world for this moment. She found that her heart was beating much too quickly, and she forced herself to close her eyes and remind herself that *que será será*, and that, after all, a thousand years from now—Following these incantations she opened her eyes and looked around her. They were parked in a dusty narrow alley, surrounded by earthen walls. Off to her left she saw the high, lacquer-tiled roofs of what had to be the Drum Tower. Between this and the bus lay a maze of mud-and-straw walls, interrupted here and there by alleys leading into a mysterious interior. There was no barbershop; in fact, there were no shops to be seen at all, there were only walls.

No panic please, she told herself, and smiled at a small roundfaced child who grinned back at her. She called to Mr. Li, "I'm going to take some pictures of children, I'll catch up with you in a minute." Having said this she knelt in the dust and began dramatically snapping pictures with a camera that was completely empty of film. As the others moved away down the dusty lane she slipped into the nearest alley and, with several of the children trailing her, began to look for a barbershop.

She was soon completely lost and gave herself up to the luxurious feeling of being on her own again, free of the group but cherishing too the assumption that somewhere— somehow—there would be a way out of this maze of clay-colored walls. In the meantime it was fascinating to be inside them instead of looking at them from the outside: to glance into dark rooms and tiny courtyards, assess the herbs hung in doorways to dry, watch children squatting in the dust to draw figures with a stick or a stone. She passed two ancient men playing cards, one of them with a marvelous wisp of goatee on his chin, like a mandarin; she smiled and nodded to them and received courtly bows in return. Threading her way through one lane after another she turned left, then right, stopping now and then to take a pretend-picture of a flower, a doorway, a child, until at last she entered a much broader alley to find herself virtually under the roofs of the Drum Tower but still inside the compound's walls.

Here at least there were markets: stalls and shops carved into the clay wall behind them, and people, far too many people. She walked slowly down this wider road, nodding and smiling to passersby, trying not to notice the number who came to their doors to watch her, or that slight edginess she felt at being so conspicuous. She passed a bicycle repair shop; she passed a stall in which an ancient sewing machine had been installed, and then a vendor of steaming noodles.

And then—quite suddenly—she found herself passing a barbershop.

She tried not to stare. Her quick glance noted an exterior of crumbling adobe that matched the wall into which it was set, a large, very dusty glass window, an open door and a dim interior filled with men. Only the chair placed near the window identified it, and the man with clippers bent over his customer in the chair.

Here is a barbershop, thought Mrs. Pollifax, *but not where I thought it would be, or where Carstairs and Bishop thought it would be, either.*

She continued past it, glanced into a shop filled with women working at a long workbench, and finding neither an exit from this alley or another barbershop she stopped. She thought, "If it's not Guo Musu in there—well, that's why I was chosen, isn't it? Because I stand up well under police interrogations?"

But for a moment she thought indignantly of Carstairs and Bishop, neither of whom realized the quantities of people on the move in China in the daytime, and the total lack of privacy anywhere. People on the street, people crowded into a barbershop . . . they had certainly not considered the effect of an American tourist plunging in among the crowds to ask for information. It was outrageous and it might prove suicidal, but she was going to have to go into that shop.

She turned and retraced her steps to its door.

A dozen men seated along the wall gaped at her as she walked inside. She called out, "Does anyone here speak English?" The barber was intent on guiding clippers around the ears of his customer; he had scarcely glanced up at her arrival and her heart sank at the lack of response. She began again. "Does anyone here—"

The barber lifted his head and looked at her. "I speak a little." He was a nondescript, sallow man, his face devoid of expression.

"I'm so glad," she said with an enthusiasm she didn't feel. "I'm lost. I wonder if you could come to the door—" here she pointed, "and show me the way to the Drum Tower?"

The man spoke to his companions in his own language; heads nodded and the smiles blossomed so ardently that for a minute she feared they might all jump up to help her. But the barber had put down his clippers and he joined her alone in the doorway.

"Please—come outside," she said in a low voice. "Are you Guo Musu?"

He stiffened. "How is this, please," he whispered, "that you know my name?"

They were being watched with interest by a circle of bystanders in the alley, and by the men behind them in the barbershop. In spite of their being out of earshot she knew that she must be careful and protect this man, whether he helped her or not. She asked, "Which way to the Drum Tower?"

Automatically he pointed in the direction she'd been heading; she hoped this gesture established authenticity, but it was going to be difficult to remember appropriate gestures while she talked. "There isn't much time," she said quickly. "Your brother Chang, who reached Hong Kong safely, said you could tell me where the camp is located that you lived in for three years. The labor camp somewhere in Xinjiang Province."

"Chang!" he exclaimed. "Labor camp?"

Damn, she thought, and deplored this lack of time and privacy, *he's going to need time to adjust to this, the shock couldn't have been greater if I announced that I came from the moon.* "I'm visiting your country," she told him politely. "We're enjoying Xian very much. We saw Ban Po Village this morning, and tomorrow we visit the tomb of—"

Amusement flickered in his eyes; she had underestimated him. He said, "And you have somehow found me to ask—"

"I know what you think," she told him frankly. "You could be arrested for giving me this information but I can also be arrested for asking you."

An ironic smile crossed his face.

"I'm American," she told him. "It's Americans who would like to know."

"Americans," he repeated, turning the word over on his tongue. "And just what do you expect of me?" There was a very real irony in his voice now.

She said earnestly, "What I thought—what I hoped—I bought an atlas this morning in Xian, with Xinjiang Province on page thirty-eight. Let me show you." She turned to page thirty-eight and handed it to him. "If you decide to trust me I thought we might walk a little—away from your shop and your neighbors—and I could hand you a pen."

He looked at her, studying her with curiosity and interest. The irony slowly receded; he said at last, quietly, "I will walk with you to the end of the road and show you the way to the Drum Tower."

"Oh thank you," she gasped, adding quickly, "You're very kind."

He said politely, "Not at all."

As they walked he glanced down at the map of Xinjiang Province, whereas Mrs. Pollifax glanced back, relieved to see that only a few of the smaller children followed, but at a distance. Nearing the end of the alley he looked up from the atlas and met her gaze. Wordlessly she offered him the pen, leaning closer to him so that no one would see. He gravely accepted it.

"I'll keep talking," she told him as he made a mark on the map, and without watching him she began a panto-mime of gestures and smiles. After a moment he slipped the atlas back into her hand, and she slid it into her purse.

Bringing out her identical copy she said, "In case any one saw us—"

His eyes widened in astonishment.

"No, this is a duplicate," she said, presenting it to him with a bow. "Look at page thirty-eight and you'll see."

He turned to that page, and she saw his relief. "Please take it," she told him. "As a gift. For showing me the way to the Drum Tower."

"For showing you the way to the Drum Tower," he repeated, and suddenly smiled, showing a number of teeth capped in steel. "And Chang?" he asked, his irony exquis-ite now. "He is well?"

"I am told he is very well," she said, smiling back at him, and suddenly she was aware of the immensity of what he had dared to do for her, and she seized the book he held and wrote her name in it. "Now each of us knows," she told him. "It's only fair. We're hostages now to each other."

"But there was no need for that," he told her gently.

Startled, she said, "Oh?"

"Your eyes speak for you, which is why I do this," he said. "I think it is possible that you also follow The Way."

She had forgotten that he was Buddhist. "I seek," she acknowledged softly, "but sometimes—oh, in very strange ways."

His smile was warm. "But there are no strange ways, *xianben*—only the search."

"Ah," she said with a catch of breath, and for a long moment they gazed at each other and she was mute, deeply touched by a recognition, a tenderness between them. She said at last, very softly, "Thank you, Mr. Guo, and—please—may you have long life and double happiness."

He nodded and walked away, once again a sallow nondescript man, no doubt wearing an ironic smile for the comrades who moved eagerly toward him. She watched him hold up the atlas she'd given him, and as his neighbors drew close to examine it she left. Presently she was mounting the steps to the Drum Tower.

Mr. Li was waiting at the entrance. "Where have you been?" he demanded. "Miss Bai has gone to search for you."

She only smiled at him, and moved past him.

She found the others in the small Friendship Store at the top of the building, looking into glass cases at ancient relics displayed for sale. Not one of them looked up at her entrance, and she commended her silent partner for being so controlled and disciplined an actor. But although she too concentrated on the relics with control and discipline, her thoughts remained with Guo Musu and on that curious sense of meeting that she'd experienced with him. *Nothing happens by accident*, she thought, and she knew that she would not easily forget that moment of tenderness between them.

And she had succeeded. Her job was done. She'd found and made contact with Guo Musu and there was exhilaration in this, and a sense of triumph.

They attended Chinese Opera that evening. Mrs. Pollifax, tired from the suspense and from the tensions of finding Guo Musu, found Jenny and Peter extremely irritating. In spite of being several years older, it was Jenny who seemed to be succumbing to Peter's hostile attitudes: they had moved from an early sharing of college jokes and anecdotes to a running patter of tactless criticisms of China that

Mrs. Pollifax found deplorable. She had already overheard a few whispered flippancies about Mr. Li, and only that morning they'd been giggling about the questions Iris had asked at the cloisonné factory's tea and briefing.

Now it was the Shaanxi local opera that met with their unkind laughter.

Mrs. Pollifax herself was entranced. The theater was shabby and the audience in dull work clothes, but the stage shone like a jewel with the brilliance of the costumes— color for the eye at last, she thought, as she feasted on it. Mr. Li had explained to them that the ancient tale was in serial form and had begun three nights ago; it would last four hours tonight, but they would depart at intermission. Mrs. Pollifax found no problems at all in following it: the gestures were stylized but the meaning of each one, coupled with the droll and vivid expressions on the actors' faces needed no words of explanation. There was a marvelous humor in the story, and she laughed along with the audience without the slightest idea of what was being said.

Jenny, however, was not content with this and demanded of Mr. Li a translation of every word spoken, after which she would repeat his explanation in a loud voice for the rest of them.

"So this guy—the one in black," she was saying, "has come down from heaven to avenge the death of—which one, Mr. Li?"

"Get a load of the singing!" interrupted Peter, laughing. "Straight through the nasal passages, vibrating all the sinuses!"

Jenny giggled. "Not to mention how the princess sniffles into her sleeves, the one in bright red?"

Ugly Americans, thought Mrs. Pollifax sadly, and was about to speak to them when George Westrum surprised and impressed her by turning around and doing it first.

"Look here," he growled, "you're not giving this a chance, and you're being damned rude, too."

Mrs. Pollifax glanced around and saw that Jenny had the grace to blush but Peter's face only turned cold and stony again. They stopped their chattering and Mrs. Pollifax returned to the opera, but something had gone out of the evening. She realized that the first rift had appeared in their group, and the embarrassment of it hung in the air, an embarrassment for themselves, for Mr. Li, for China, and for Peter and Jenny. It was not a comfortable way to feel, thought Mrs. Pollifax, and when they left at the intermission there were no comments about the opera on their way back to the hotel. The silence was awkward, and only Iris and Mrs. Pollifax called out good night to Jenny and Peter.

She had been alone in her room for only a few minutes when the door opened, startling her. She turned her head to see Peter walk in without knocking and she was appalled at this breach of manners; not even the assumption that he might have come to apologize dampened her sense of outrage. She said angrily, "Whether you realize it or not, Peter, it's customary to knock."

He stood there, arrogant, cold, and sulky. He closed the door behind him and without paying her words any attention he walked across the room and tucked the curtains more securely around the air-conditioner. Only then did he turn and say quietly, in a voice she'd never heard from him before, "I've come to ask if you made contact with Guo Musu today."

⊡⊡⊡⊡⊡⊡⊡⊡⊡⊡⊡⊡⊡⊡⊡⊡⊡⊡⊡⊡ 7

MRS. POLLIFAX STARED AT HIM INCREDULOUSLY. "YOU?"
she gasped. "*You!*"

He stood silent, watching her, waiting.

"You're too young," she flung at him. "You're only
twenty-two, how could you possibly be one of Cars—"
She stopped.

"One of Carstairs' people," he finished for her.

She stared at him in shock, her mind spinning in an
effort to adjust: *not* Joe Forbes, *not* Malcolm Styles, *not*
George Westrum. She said, feeling her way toward something concrete, "You can't possibly speak Chinese or—"

"Fluently. Mandarin as well as several dialects."

"There was that grandmother—"

"Oh yes, that grandmother," he said with a faint smile.

"Born in Kansas City, Missouri, actually, and the closest she's come to China is Mah-Jongg."

"What's more I've *disliked* you," she told him angrily. "I didn't realize how much until you walked in just now without knocking. Spoiled, sulky, unappreciative—"

"That good, huh?"

Mrs. Pollifax began to laugh. "I see . . . yes. All right—*very* good, and I'm acting like an idiot." She held out her hand to him. "I'm sorry."

His handclasp was firm. "It was a shock for me when I first saw you too," he conceded politely. "I won't say where it was, but definitely it was a shock."

"That bad, huh?" she mimicked, smiling at him. "Then shall we start all over again before getting on with the job?"

"If there *is* a job," he said quietly. "Look, the suspense has been damn hard to handle, I didn't see any barbershop at all near the Drum Tower."

She nodded. "Then I'm delighted to tell you that there was a barbershop and a Guo Musu, too."

"My God," he said, staring at her. "Where?"

"Hidden away in that maze of alleys."

"But were you able to—did he—"

She nodded. "It's in my purse, excuse me."

"*What's* in your purse?"

She reached across him to the bedside table, groped for the atlas and brought it out. "Page thirty-eight," she said, opening it and handing it to him.

He stared at it in amazement. "Where on earth did you get a Chinese atlas?"

"In the department store this morning," she told him. "*Quite* by accident. I pointed to what I thought would be a book of poems and they handed me this instead. It was a miracle."

As he leaned over page thirty-eight Peter's face was no

longer impassive. "It's a miracle all right," he said, and glanced up at her. "Have you looked at this? Guo's not only marked the location of the labor camp but he's added notes."

"Notes?" she echoed, and Guo's face returned to her again, and that moment of sharing, of knowing. "He did that for us, too?" she said, with a catch in her voice.

"I'll say!" He showed her the page, excited now. "He's pinpointed the labor camp halfway between Urumchi, where we go tomorrow, and Turfan—just off the main highroad over the Tian Shan mountains. But what's even more fantastic, he's scribbled a footnote explaining the circle he's drawn, he says it marks a Red Army barracks some six or eight miles from the labor camp." He looked at her and shook his head. "How did you manage all this? You were missing for only about forty-five minutes this afternoon. I mean, you're one hell of a surprise."

"Thank you," she said.

"No, I mean it," he told her. "To get all this in minutes from an absolute stranger? Since reaching Xian I've been feeling damnably humbled, wondering how on earth I'd have managed it. I wanted to, you know, I insisted on doing it myself but Carstairs refused. This morning I realized I'd have behaved like a bull in a tea shop. Spoken Chinese probably, alarmed Guo Musu thoroughly, even given the whole show away and gotten nowhere. How did you do it?"

"It's probably why they sent me," said Mrs. Pollifax modestly. "The Chinese do have a deep respect for their elders, after all, and I tend to look quite harmless."

He grinned. "That's for sure—you fooled *me*. And now—" He hesitated, staring down at page thirty-eight. "It's incredible but I think we're in business at last. I can even get down to some serious planning now. Amazing."

She smiled at him. "Good—but did *you* by any chance search my suitcase last night?"

He looked at her blankly. "Search your—why should I want to search your suitcase?"

"Oh," she said with a sinking heart. "It wasn't you, then?"

"No of course not." Peter looked shocked. "Are you sure?"

"Oh yes. Somebody did. Was yours?"

He shook his head. "No, I take the usual precautions. I'd have known right away." His brows drew together into a frown. "I don't get it, who would do such a thing, and why? And why *you?*"

"It was done very professionally," she told him, "and it wouldn't have been noticeable at all if I didn't have my own way of packing, too. The lock wasn't picked, and everything was left in order—but not the right order." His scowl had turned into such a look of alarm that she added softly, "Don't look so jarred, it was probably some sort of random security check." She didn't think at all that it was a security check, but she saw no point in worrying Peter just now when he had his plans to make. "In any case," she told him cheerfully, "I think we should put it aside for the moment, there being other things to think about, don't you agree? Which leads me to a question I've been waiting for some time to ask you. With enormous curiosity."

She had succeeded in distracting him; he smiled. "Be my guest and ask, but I'll bet I know what it is."

She smiled back at him. "I'm sure you do: the one detail no one's mentioned, and which didn't seep through to me until too late to ask. You're going to be escorting our friend Mr. Wang—X—out of the country, aren't you." She didn't even bother to make it a question.

He nodded.

"Then as a bona fide member of a bona fide guided

tour, allowed to visit China as a tourist, how are you ever
going to manage to vanish from the tour and gain freedom
for your very risky undercover work? I can't believe that
you'll just bolt. You wouldn't have a chance, would you?"

He shook his head. "Not a chance in a million. No,
there'll be an accident."

"Accident," she repeated, watching his face intently.
"What kind?"

"That's up to me," he told her. "I've a few ideas
boiling around in my head but it depends on a lot of
factors like terrain and circumstances and timing. I'll be
killed," he added casually.

"Killed," she repeated, and waited.

"In such a way there'll be no trace of a body," he
explained, adding soberly, "and it's growing on me fast
that your help is going to be very much needed."

"I see," she said musingly. "Yes, it would have to be
that, of course. The *only* way to vanish into China."

"Yes—become a non-person. Without the Sepos in hot
pursuit. A dead person."

She shivered. "Not easy."

"No."

"And from the vitamins and dried food I'm carrying I
deduce you'll be heading for the mountains?"

He nodded. "There's been the feeble hope that another
route might open up, but I don't think it will."

"Very *high* mountains," she said quietly. "And cold
ones. Surely not through Tibet?"

"No, we can head around the Taklamakan desert toward
Khotan and a pass over the Karakaroms."

"The very thought chills me," she admitted. "Literally
as well as figuratively."

He nodded. "That's where I'll need your help, too; you
can help me find warm clothing and carry some of it in
your suitcase when mine's full."

"Like what?" she asked, and reached for paper and pencil, glad to move her thoughts toward the practical.

He frowned as he concentrated. "What I did smuggle in is small stuff. I've got thermal underwear, two heavy ski masks rolled up, fake papers, and a heavy sweater. The windbreaker jacket I brought has a second one zipped inside it. I've knives, flashlights and batteries, a good compass hidden in my camera, topographical maps, complete medicine kit right down to snake serum, and two collapsible canvas bags for water—"

"Plus the chocolate I brought, the dried foods, and vitamins—"

"Yes. And now what's needed is more of the big stuff. Blankets and sheepskins—anything that can be cut into vests and coats. We're heading tomorrow into nomad country where there ought to be sheepskins in the bazaars or Friendship Stores. Buy whatever you find, you can refuse to have it mailed home for you until we get to Beijing, make up some sort of story, rope whatever you find to the outside of your suitcase and keep it with you."

"Right," she said crisply, noting this down on paper.

"In the meantime," he added with a crooked smile, "I have my Mao cap and jacket, and they were very nearly top priority, believe me, because I shall have to become as Chinese as a native soon."

"How on earth did you learn fluent Chinese at such an age?" she asked. "It's unexpected."

"Very weirdly," he told her. "When I was into my freshman year at Harvard—yeah, Harvard," he admitted with a grin, "I started out hanging around bars in Chinatown in Boston. Coincidence? I don't know. And I began picking up the language bit by bit—with an ease that staggered me. Coincidence? I don't know. By the time I graduated from Harvard I could read and write Mandarin, and was already into dialects, and it's not true, either, that I've just finished my senior year. I'm in graduate school now—their Far Asian studies department—or was, until I took off to get in shape for this.''

"And Carstairs?"

He grinned. "No, it was Bishop. I met *him* in a Chinatown bar in Boston, or perhaps—who knows?—he arranged to meet me there because he'd heard of me. A setup maybe.''

She smiled. "Quite possibly. And here we are."

"Yes. And now I have this," he said, looking down at the atlas with astonishment. "I'll take it along to my room and figure kilometers from the map I brought, and do some calculations.''

"Did anyone see you come into my room?" asked Mrs. Pollifax, remembering her searched suitcase, and still uneasy about it.

He shook his head. "The hall was empty." He thought a minute. "If anyone's in the hall when I make my exit I'll say I came to borrow a drinking glass. But tell me first—I'm curious—what was Guo Musu like?''

She told him, describing the barbershop and their meeting, and as she talked she became aware of several quick, perceptive glances directed at her, as if he understood much more than she was saying, and for this she was grateful.

When she had finished he nodded. "I wish I could have talked with him. It's been terribly frustrating," he added, with a rush of boyish candor. "The opera tonight, for instance. I really hated Jenny's running commentary when I could understand every word for myself, and I came near to hating her for demeaning it. I've also overheard and understood everything that Mr. Li and Miss Bai talk about together, and I feel like a bloody eavesdropper. Mr. Li,'' he said ruefully, "doesn't think very highly of me either.''

He stood up. "I'll go along now and study this map more closely."

Rising too she said, "It might be a good idea for us to become a shade friendlier inside the group. In case we're seen talking together, as we'll surely have to do from time to time."

"Good," he said, with a grin. "I'll begin sitting next to you at meals occasionally, and show signs of thawing. And look," he added almost shyly, "you've been great. I'm awfully glad to have finally met you. *Really* met you, I mean."

She smiled at him warmly. "That goes for me, too." As he moved to open the door she said, "Hold it a moment," and ducked into her bathroom. "Your water glass," she reminded him.

He whistled. "You really are a pro! I forgot, damn it." And glass in hand he made his exit.

⌐⌐⌐⌐⌐⌐⌐⌐⌐⌐⌐⌐⌐⌐⌐⌐⌐⌐⌐⌐ **8**

THEY DROVE THE NEXT MORNING TO THE TOMB OF CHINA'S first emperor Qin Shi Huang, and if this had once promised to be the highlight of sightseeing for her, Mrs. Pollifax now found it difficult to think of anything but Peter's visit to her room last night.

For one thing, the very magnitude of the job that he'd been given nearly overwhelmed her: to devise his own death, to rescue a stranger from a labor camp and then travel what had to be hundreds of miles over desert and cruel mountain passes seemed incredible. The man whom Peter had been sent to rescue had to be very important indeed, she was thinking, and here, too, she decided there must be a great deal that Carstairs had not told her.

And then there was Peter himself . . . She still marveled

at his being the agent sent in with her, and she was not at
all displeased, but she wished that he'd not forgotten that
drinking glass. It was a trivial omission, but it reminded
her of his youth and the fact that this was probably his first
job, and if so, a massive one. He was certainly a good
actor, and he was intelligent. From her impressions of him
she guessed there was a natural exuberance in him about
what lay ahead, and that this would have been the quality
that captured Carstairs' attention, for if she trembled for
Peter, she was absolutely certain that Peter did not tremble
for himself. Behind the impassive face that had softened
only slightly last night she had glimpsed that sort of loner
who had to climb mountains because they were there, as
the saying went, and for whom danger was addicting, and
ordinary life puzzling. It was the stuff of which the T. E.
Lawrences and Richard Halliburtons were made, she mused,
embryonic now in a cool twenty-two-year-old, and obviously invaluable for this particular job.

But as an agent, she thought, he should never have
forgotten that water glass.

And this, she mused, was perhaps another reason why
she'd been chosen to accompany Peter: to keep an eye on
him and to steady him. It amused her to remember that this
was precisely what she'd done by instinct last evening
when he'd looked so alarmed about her suitcase being
searched: she had reassured and distracted him, hiding her
own alarm. Carstairs, she thought, must have done some
rare chuckling when he tossed the two of them into this
maelstrom—he was no fool about people—but at the moment she wished she might have a few indignant words
with him. Obviously, her job in China was not to end in
Xian, after all. It might even be just beginning.

She glanced toward the front of the minibus at Peter,
who was seated next to Malcolm this morning, as if he'd
decided to divest himself of Jenny for the day, and she

wondered idly what they were talking about. The two guides sat in front of them, with Miss Bai occasionally interrupting her conversation with Mr. Li to pick up the microphone and point out a field of workers, a commune, or a factory. And then—abruptly—they were pulling into the parking lot of the archaeological site, and ahead lay a broad courtyard framed by low-lying buildings, the largest of which resembled an airplane hangar.

"No cameras allowed," called out Mr. Li.

"No—no pictures," echoed Miss Bai. "We meet here again in one hour, the Friendship Store on the left, a film theater next it showing history of this remarkable discovery, and soda pop to be found in souvenir building."

It was Joe Forbes with whom Mrs. Pollifax strolled toward the hangarlike building that had been erected over the remarkable discoveries. "But this isn't the tomb itself?" he asked pleasantly.

"I don't believe they've even started on the tomb yet," she told him. "These are the burial figures found on the periphery. He took an entire army to the grave with him, but mercifully not a live one, which I do think was kind of him, and very enlightened."

"Another discovery," he quipped, "when a factory was planned?"

"According to the guidebook, this time it was commune workers digging a well." *Pleasantries from behind plexiglass*, she thought, darting a glance at his pleasant, smiling, never-changing face, but knowing now that he wasn't Carstairs' man she felt little need to probe the mystery behind his lack of personality; there probably was no mystery at all, she decided; some people were simply born bland.

They walked together into the building, where Mrs. Pollifax promptly moved to the railing that separated them from the digging site, and here she caught her breath. She

had been certain that she knew what to expect; she had
studiously looked up photographs but now she realized that
they'd been taken out of context, mere pictures in a maga-
zine lacking environment and reality. The sheer impact of
what she saw stunned her: hundreds of life-sized men
standing below her in the broad trenches that honeycombed
the earth floor, men like gray ghosts waiting patiently at
attention, hundreds of them in battle formation lined up in
rows as far as the eye could see, each face different and
individual with here and there a hand lifted or a head
turned slightly as if to listen. Silent and waiting they filled
the hall, so alive in gesture and stance that surely,
she thought, they must be breathing as they stood there,
liberated from the earth that had held them for nearly two
thousand years.

Malcolm, coming to stand beside her, said simply, "My
God."

She smiled, liking Malcolm. "It's a mighty emperor
who goes to his grave with—how many?" she asked.

"The latest count is five hundred terra-cotta warriors,
six war chariots, and twenty-four horses, with thousands
more expected."

Iris, joining them, whistled, and the three of them stood
there, staring down into the trenches, absorbed and awed
until Mrs. Pollifax, recovering, began to be aware of a
very odd sensation of tension flowing between Malcolm
and Iris. Strange, she thought, standing between them. She
glanced curiously at Malcolm, but he was staring at the
figures below; she looked at Iris, but she too was staring
straight ahead, her lips still pursed in a whistle, and then
George Westrum came up to claim Iris and the tension
snapped. But for just a moment Mrs. Pollifax felt that
she'd stumbled into a kind of energy-force field, and since
she was not accustomed to picking up vibrations so strongly

it left her puzzled. *Perhaps this place is a little haunted,* she thought, and wondered what had happened to her.

Iris and George walked away together and Malcolm wandered on, his sketchbook in hand. When Mrs. Pollifax resumed strolling it was Peter who fell in with her.

"Seems a good time to get friendlier," he said with his wry half-smile. "We leave for Urumchi late this afternoon and I've been doing my homework."

"Productive?" she asked, trying not to look eager in case anyone was watching.

"Definitely." His voice was crisp, with an undercurrent of excitement. "It looks good—ideas begin to blossom. Nothing's jelled yet but I'm absolutely certain now that the thing can be pulled off, all of it." With a nod toward the excavations he added, "What do you think?"

"Incredible. Spooky, even, they feel so alive."

"He was a bit of a bastard, that first emperor," Peter said pleasantly. "Burned books. Executed his friends. Made some pretty severe laws. But," he added, "the laws he made were the first the country ever had, and one of them was to banish feudalism, even if it did pop back after his death. He pulled a lot of warring states together and gave the country shape and unity, and without all that China might never have tamed the *Xiong nu* during the next dynasty."

"Tamed who?"

"*Hsiung-nu*—the horse people, the nomads from the steppes who swarmed through the passes of the Altai and Tian Shan ranges to attack . . . Mongols and Turkic people. That's where we're heading later today, you know, into frontier country. Urumchi, Turfan, the Tarim Basin, the Tian Shans, the Taklamakan desert. Back in 221 B.C. it was China's wild west, the far frontier."

"Genghis Khan, perhaps?"

"Yes, eventually. What riders they must have been,

sweeping down from the mountains into the desert, with towns changing hands at the drop of a crossbow!''

"And has it been tamed now?" she asked, picturing what he spoke of in her mind.

"It's not been made an Autonomous Region for nothing," he told her. "I gather the central government still has its problems there and has had to make a few compromises. Not easy trying to organize nomads into communes, and Moslems into good Communists. A great number of ethnic groups live there—it was the Silk Road, after all!—the Uyghurs being in the majority."

"Weegurs?" she repeated.

"Yes, but spelled U-y-g-h-u-r, which may give you an idea of the language you'll meet there, most of the words being pronounced with strange gargling sounds. For instance the word for good-bye is *hox*, which you pronounce *horrssh*, and *aromat* is thank you, but comes out *rock-met*, slightly gargled. In any case, Mao tried to solve the Uyghur majority by sending thousands of Chinese into the province to settle among them, but basically it's Moslem country and they've had their share of incidents, so-called.''

"Uprisings?" asked Mrs. Pollifax in surprise.

"Passive resistance would probably describe it better. In fact, something like sixty thousand Kazakhs simply left China in 1962, going over the border into Soviet Kazakhstan."

"How absolutely fascinating," she said. "I wish Mr. Li could be this informative."

Peter shook his head. "You can't blame Mr. Li," he said soberly. "From his age I'd guess he was brought up during the Cultural Revolution, when education went into an ice age. You probably know more about his country and its history than he does, though he's learning fast." He shook his head again. "These abrupt changes must have been psychological hell for people, at one point raiding

monasteries, closing schools, and sending intellectuals into
the fields or to prison; the next decade opening the schools,
retrieving teachers and scientists from the rice fields, and
restoring the same buildings that were mutilated. It has a
certain Alice-In-Wonderland quality, you know? Mao may
have been a brilliant revolutionary, but he sure as hell
lacked consistency for the long run. Oops, here comes
Jenny,'' he said. ''I'd better mend my political fences and
talk to her. See you later,'' he added quickly, and strolled
back toward Jenny, his face emptied of expression again.

In the afternoon they visited Huaching Hot Springs
Guesthouse, from which Chiang Kai-shek had escaped
capture by the Communists, leaving his teeth behind. It
was a very charming place, with ponds and arched bridges,
but Mrs. Pollifax only felt uncomfortably hot; her feet
were tired and she sat down as often as possible and as
close to the water as possible. Besides, she thought crossly,
Chiang Kai-shek might have escaped from a window to
climb the mountain behind his room, but he'd only been
captured and eventually released again. Of much more
interest to her was the young Communist who had hurried
to Xian to negotiate with Chiang once he was captured.
The young man's name had been Chou En-lai, and Mrs.
Pollifax had long since succumbed to Chou's personality
from seeing him on television. She completely understood
the reaction to his death in 1976 when the people defied
Mao and the police to pour into Beijing's Tian An Men
Square and mourn Chou in their own way. It had been a
spontaneous outpouring of national grief and love and
worry that had been conspicuously missing when Mao died
eight months later.

She was seated on a bench thinking about this when
Peter strolled up the path and sat down beside her. His
face impassive he said, ''Jenny's gone to find a ladies'

room so I've got to talk fast. Quick—have you pencil and paper?'' She was amused to see that he was speaking out of the corner of his mouth, just like a film gangster.

She nodded and dug into her purse, bringing out her memo pad.

''I've been talking to Mr. Li about what we see in Urumchi, and it sounds good, as if we'll be visiting all the right places, but when he confers with you—and he will, because you're leader, remember?—make sure we visit the Kazakhs up in the grasslands *after* our overnight stay in Turfan. You can't possibly know what I mean, and there's no time to explain so just write it down, okay?''

Mrs. Pollifax wrote TURFAN, SEE FIRST. ''Is there a name for the grasslands?''

''Yes, take a look at your Markham Tour brochure if you brought it—''

''Didn't.''

''The grasslands have always been a part of their regular tours here, and we've got to insist on them, but *after* visiting Turfan. If I remember correctly the brochure reads''—he closed his eyes and quoted—'' 'See the color-ful Kazakh Minority Peoples demonstrate their superb horsemanship. A nomadic people, they live in summer in yurts on the grasslands of the Tian Shan mountains.' And,'' he added, ''we simply *must* go there last.''

''I wonder what reason I could possibly give Mr. Li for this,'' she asked pensively.

''Tell him *something*. Tell him you've heard how hot Turfan is . . . Well, it is,'' he said. ''It's five hundred feet below sea level.''

''Below!'' she exclaimed.

''Yes you'll find it listed on maps as the *Turfan Depression*. It's also an oasis in the desert, and *hot*. You can tell Mr. Li you're feeling the heat, or someone is, and it would be lovely to cool off in the mountains after Turfan.''

He smiled faintly. "You seem to manage okay. As leader you've got clout—use it. And if it's any help," he added, "Jenny seems to be getting tourist tummy, or Montezuma's Revenge, or dysentery, whatever the current word is."

"Oh dear!"

"Yes." He nodded and as Jenny appeared from between two ancient buildings he added flatly, "But it's *absolutely necessary* we go to Turfan first. Totally. I'll explain why when we get to Urumchi."

"I'll look forward to that," she told him dryly, with the distinct feeling it would be much kinder if she avoided hearing that explanation.

It was a six-hour flight to Urumchi. The two-engine prop plane fairly bulged with passengers, a few even seated on their luggage in the aisles. A hostess occasionally negotiated her way among them, passing out candies or cups of tea, but for dinner they landed at Lanzhou and dined in an echoing hall of the air terminal, handed warm moist wash cloths as they entered, and warm moist cloths at the meal's end. The paper napkins, noticed Mrs. Pollifax, were steadily shrinking in size; they had not been large in Canton, but they were now approaching the shape of her memo pad, and were slippery as well. Following dinner they returned to the plane and in the hours before darkness Mrs. Pollifax looked down at stark, barren mountain ranges, golden-brown in color like dark honey illuminated by the sun's gold. Occasionally—surprising her—she saw terraces carved out of a mountainside, forming patterns like ripples in a pond but with no sign of villages or of human life anywhere in the incredibly empty landscape.

China, she decided, looking down at it, was all terra-cotta and dusty jade. Everywhere. Only the shapes changed, and the shades of beige and brown, and the presence or absence of any green at all.

It was night when they landed in Urumchi, and well past ten o'clock. Having said good-bye to Miss Bai at the Xian air terminal there was now a Mr. Kan waiting for them here, and while still in the air terminal Mrs. Pollifax placed herself squarely in front of Mr. Li and reminded him that she was group leader. "When do we discuss plans for Urumchi?" she asked.

If Mr. Li was surprised by this sudden aggressiveness, he concealed it. "In the morning perhaps?" he suggested. "Mr. Kan will tell us what he's arranged."

"No," said Mrs. Pollifax firmly. "Tell him tonight, please, that we all want to visit Turfan *before* we go to the Kazakh grasslands. I hear that Turfan is very hot, and we'd prefer the mountains later, to cool off."

"Cool off!" he repeated, and laughed merrily at the phrase.

"Yes—do please insist on it before any plans are made final."

"You wish Turfan soon," he said, assimilating this.

"Yes. Oh yes—definitely." From the blank look that came and went on Mr. Li's face she received the distinct impression that while he spoke English well he did not understand it with equal ease. "Turfan first," she repeated, and was made more comfortable by a confirming flash of comprehension in his gaze. *He saves face,* she thought as she climbed into the waiting minibus. *How much has he understood of our prattlings? How much would I understand if people spoke rapidly, injecting slang words, and in different accents?*

Once again the hotel was nearly an hour's drive out of town, but this time there were no complaints: there was an intimacy about the *Yannan* that had been missing in the Canton hotel's oversized Art Deco vulgarity, and in the Xian hotel's stark Russian frugality. For one thing there was only a very modest fishpond in the lobby, and through an opened french door a smaller, brighter dining hall could be seen. The guest rooms were at ground level, elevated a few steps above the lobby; Mrs. Pollifax found her own room spacious and cool-looking. Its walls were white, and on one of them hung a very charming watercolor, an original, with a subtly Turkish flavor to it. Obviously new and interesting influences had entered Xinjiang Province.

But although it was nearly eleven o'clock Mrs. Pollifax felt restless, and while she waited for her suitcase to arrive at her door she gravitated toward the lobby, passing the small gift counter on the way. It had been opened for their arrival—a young woman presided over it—and Iris and George were leaning over the counter examining its treasures. In the lobby she found Malcolm sitting on the edge of the goldfish pond. "Real fish," he told her, pointing. "How are you doing?"

"Surprisingly well so far," she told him.

"Jenny has a touch of traveler's tummy. I've given her two of my pills," he said. "Anyone else, do you know?"

"Not to my knowledge," she told him, "but doubtless there'll be more. It's my theory that somewhere along the line there's usually one rebellious new employee in a kitchen who just can't understand why the water has to be boiled for foreigners, and so they don't. One has to count on that, it's human nature."

He looked amused. "Very experienced of you—about human nature, I mean. And since Jenny's been drinking nothing but boiled water—"

"So-called."

"—it's a very rational explanation. If somewhat alarming," he added, his glance moving to Iris, who was walking toward them looking excited, with George following behind her, smiling.

"Look," she cried, holding out a hand, "just see what George insisted on buying for me!" In her palm lay a disc of antique white jade, intricately carved by hand. She was radiant as she displayed it.

"How exquisite," breathed Mrs. Pollifax, bending over it.

"Lovely," said Malcolm, giving it a brief glance and then looking at Iris.

Iris turned pink. "It's *very* old," she said almost defiantly.

Jenny called from the hallway, "Any suitcases yet?"

"How are you feeling?" called Malcolm.

Jenny walked over to join them and he made room for her on the wall of the fishpond. "Better, thanks, but I should never have stashed those pills in my suitcase, we don't see our luggage that often. Thanks for bailing me out, Malcolm. What's that?" she asked Iris.

"White jade, isn't it gorgeous?"

The wide glass doors swung open now, and Mr. Li, Mr. Kan, two hotel workers, and Joe Forbes appeared with their luggage.

Iris said, "That's what I've been waiting for—good night everyone, see you in the morning! George, thanks so *very* much—see you!"

George Westrum, looking somewhat startled, tugged at his baseball cap, lingered a minute, and then drifted away, too.

Jenny said, "Excuse me," and followed the men and the luggage down the hall.

Mrs. Pollifax, leaning comfortably against the fishpond, said, "I'm so glad to see Iris given a present, wasn't she excited? I have the impression that she's not received many gifts in her life."

Malcolm said calmly, "She'll be receiving a good many of them in the future."

Startled, Mrs. Pollifax said, "From George, do you mean?"

"No, not George," he said, and then, aware of her

scrutiny he added, "or didn't I mention that I'm psychic at times?"

"No, you didn't," she told him sternly."You only said that you live with talking mice."

"The two are not synonymous," he said dryly, "but I can be quite psychic at times. It comes in flashes, and I frequently get very clear intuitions about people. How are you on the subject?"

"Oh, a believer of course," she said. "How can one be otherwise? As a matter of fact I once spent several days with a Rumanian gypsy—a queen of the gypsies, actually—who had the gift of second sight, and who—" She stopped, aware that Innocent Tourists did not usually have their lives saved by gypsy queens when being pursued by the police through Turkey. She added lamely, "But we all have the gift, haven't we, simply covered over by rationalism and disbelief?"

He had been smiling at her discomfiture. "You must tell me more sometime about your friend the gypsy but I think I'll say good night now. Hi, Jenny," he said, as Jenny reappeared.

Jenny gave him a bright but abstracted smile, and at his departure walked over to the fishpond to sit beside Mrs. Pollifax. She said in a strangled voice, "That white jade. Did George give it to Iris?"

"Yes," said Mrs. Pollifax calmly. "Why?"

Jenny pushed out her legs and stared angrily at her blue and white sneakers. There was a long silence while she examined her shoes, scowled at them, pushed back a lock of hair, and picked a piece of lint from her skirt. "I hate that woman, I just hate her," she said furiously.

"Iris?" said Mrs. Pollifax, startled. "Why?"

Jenny turned and glared at her. "She's so bloody happy all the time, and everyone—oh, I should never *never* have come on this trip," she cried, and burst into tears.

A hotel worker, passing through the lobby to the dining hall, glanced curiously at Jenny. Mrs. Pollifax said, "Come outside a moment until you feel better." She led Jenny through the glass doors to the front of the *Yannan*, where the bus had been unloaded and was just driving away, leaving the velvety darkness bisected only by splash patterns from the lighted guest rooms. Mrs. Pollifax identified her own room by her purse standing on the windowsill. In the room next to hers she saw Peter walk over to the window and pull the curtains together. Except that if it was Peter there was something odd about his face, she noted absently.

"What did you expect from your trip?" she asked, handing Jenny a handkerchief.

"I thought—I wanted—it was supposed to—" She broke into a fresh spasm of tears. "And it—" She shoved the handkerchief back into Mrs. Pollifax's hand, turned angrily and fled back into the lobby to disappear down the hall to her room. Following slowly, Mrs. Pollifax heard a door slam shut.

Peter might be able to comfort her, she thought. Peter knew Jenny best, and might be persuaded to talk to her. Since he'd not gone to bed yet—she had, after all, seen him at his window only moments ago—she went to his door and knocked. When there was no answer she knocked again, then leaned against the door and listened. She heard no sounds of running water; she heard no sounds at all. She called his name softly, so that he would know it was she, and when even this brought no answer she stood back and stared in exasperation at the door. He was simply not responding.

Or he wasn't there.

The thought of Peter not being in his room sent a chill down her spine, which struck her as a completely irrational reaction. Moving to her own door she carried in the suitcase waiting outside it, unlocked it and extracted tooth-brush and pajamas. She thought, *He's just strolling around the grounds, not sleepy yet.*

But there had been something strange about his appearance when she'd glimpsed him in the window, something off-key that troubled her. She tried to think what it was, concentrating hard on reconstructing that moment. She realized that he'd done something to his eyes. The light behind him had thrown his face into shadow, but very definitely it had been his eyes that were different: their outer corners had been subtly drawn upward, giving him a native look. It had been Peter's shoulders and head that she'd seen in the window but the face of a Chinese.

So it's begun, she thought. *This is Xinjiang Autonomous Region, we've reached Urumchi and it's begun . . . he's gone out into the night to reconnoiter, to look for the labor camp.*

She wondered how far he would go and when he'd be back. She wondered if he'd be seen and—if he were stopped—whether his papers would pass examination, and she felt a clutch of fear for him. But it was going to be like this for the next few days, she reminded herself, culminating in his eventual death, and somehow she must remain calm.

I'd better begin doing my Yoga every morning, she thought. *Resolutely!*

9

In the morning Mr. Li knocked at her door at seven o'clock, itinerary in hand. He said, "It has been difficult, Turfan first, Mr. Kan has had to change many plans, he was up very late." He didn't laugh merrily this time but he wasn't reproachful or accusing, either, and Mrs. Pollifax felt that she was meeting the real Mr. Li for the first time. "The plan," he added, "is now as you wish."

"Come in," she told him. "You can explain it to me and then I'll make a copy and hang it in the hall for everyone to see, the way Miss Bai did in Xian."

"Excellent," he said, businesslike and efficient, and walked over to her desk to spread out the papers. "As you see, we visit many places today in Urumchi—jade-cutting factory, carpet factory, museum, free market, department store, a hospital. Tomorrow morning we leave for Turfan and stay overnight. After that the Kazakhs and the grasslands—with picnic and horsemanship—and the following day Heavenly Lake, very beautiful, before leaving to begin trip to Inner Mongolia."

"Oh *very* good," she told Mr. Li warmly. "Very good indeed, I'm so grateful to you, Mr. Li. I'll want to thank Mr. Kan, too."

"Yes," said Mr. Li, looking down at the plans with satisfaction.

When he had gone she looked at the crowded schedule and wondered how and where Peter was ever going to find the space to make his own complicated plans and arrangements. She would have preferred to knock on his door at once to make sure that he was back in the Guesthouse, and to tell him that Turfan would come first, but instead she conscientiously found a Magic Marker and made a poster of Mr. Li's schedule. Carrying it out to hang in the lobby, the first thing she saw was Peter, sound asleep in a chair. She felt so infinitely relieved at seeing him that she could have kissed him but she only tiptoed past and taped the sheet to the wall.

When she turned, his eyes were open and no longer slanted. "Busy night?" she asked with a smile.

He grinned sleepily. "You don't miss much. You guessed?"

She nodded. "Jenny was upset. I thought you could talk to her so I knocked on your door." Pointing to the itinerary she said, "Turfan tomorrow, the grasslands later."

That woke him in a hurry. "Thank God," he said fervently, and sprang out of his chair to look. "Now we're really in business," he told her, removing a memo pad from his pocket and beginning to copy it. "Look, I've got to talk to you—"

He stopped as Malcolm and then George strolled into

the lobby, followed a moment later by Joe Forbes. The doors to the dining room opened; Iris rushed in after them, upsetting a chair before she could sit down, and as Mrs. Pollifax began to attack roasted peanuts again with chopsticks Jenny walked in, her eyes still pink-rimmed, and across the table Peter winked at her. Another day had begun.

It was a crowded day. Although Peter remained upright and interested during the tours, Mrs. Pollifax was amused to notice how he dozed off during the tea-and-briefings. There were a number of these today because they preceded each inspection of a factory, and the scene was always the same: a bare utilitarian room with a photograph of Mao on the wall, a long table lined with tea cups in which lay dubious brittle twigs over which a young woman would pour boiling water from a thermos. Following an interval of five or ten minutes the tea would sink to the bottom of the cup so that the brew could be sipped without acquiring a mouth full of twigs, and the foreman or cadre would begin his talk about the factory or the workshop, halting frequently for Mr. Kan or Mr. Li to translate his words into English. When this had been done, questions were eagerly awaited. George usually wanted to know about machinery and methods, Joe Forbes asked for production figures and annoyingly checked them out on paper looking for flaws, and then Iris would begin. Mrs. Pollifax found it hilarious to watch the change in Iris when her turn came: her face lost all of its liveliness and every vestige of humor, as if knowledge was a matter too sacred for lightness. She turned deeply serious, the Conscientious Student personified in her pursuit of how women lived, what they ate and earned; her questions had a rooted intelligence behind them but they came out absurdly muddled.

Malcolm, with a quizzical twist to his brows, murmured, "Do you suppose there's a masters' thesis involved here somewhere?'' Jenny's lips thinned angrily while Peter simply dozed and missed it all.

It was during the visit to the carpet factory that Mrs. Pollifax found Peter alone at last. George was determined to buy a rug in China and have it shipped home, and he was not a man to be cheated. While the others stood around listening and yawning and sprawled across piles of rugs, Mrs. Pollifax slipped away, her interest in carpets depleted.

Wandering outside she found Peter restlessly pacing up and down the alley, pausing to run his eyes over a huge chalkboard on which words had been printed in pink and white chalk. ''Mao's thoughts for the day,'' he said, turning to her. ''Thanks for getting Turfan fixed up so quickly. I hear that originally it was to be last, so you've really saved the day.''

She waved this aside impatiently. ''Where did you go last night?''

''Let's sit on the steps,'' he suggested. ''I hiked. Walked and walked and walked. For one thing I found the Army barracks—bless Guo Musu for putting *that* on the map—and this gave me a bearing on where the labor camp has to be.''

She stared at him, appalled. ''But you must have walked *miles!*''

''Yes of course—walked, jogged, ran. All of it in total darkness, naturally, but there was only the one road to follow and I managed to stay on it. It was a pretty close connection, though, I didn't get back here until six this morning. But I also found a river, and it just *has* to be the one that flows past and around X's labor camp—I plan to follow it tonight and see.''

She shivered. ''If you find the camp will you try to make contact with X?''

''Good Lord no, just get the lay of the land,'' he said

flatly. "I won't try to reach X until I've officially disappeared."

She glanced over their itinerary. "And when—when will the—uh—disappearance happen?" The words had stuck in her throat, she couldn't think why; it seemed a simple enough question.

"At the grasslands, directly after we've visited Turfan. On Thursday."

"Thursday," she repeated, nodding. And this was Monday . . . three more days. Until he officially died, leaving no body behind. She said carefully, "Why has it been so important that we go to Turfan first?"

He waited as a workman passed, wheeling a cart filled with bricks. "To hide things there. A cache," he explained. "If you look at your map you'll find Turfan's a desert oasis four hours by car south of Urumchi, and on the same route that X and I will take as we head for the mountains. We can collect food and blankets there on our way, since I can scarcely disappear with a suitcase."

He sounded pleased; she glanced into his face and found no hint of tension or fear. "That's very clever," she told him, adding dryly, "I forgive you here and now that forgotten drinking glass."

"Forgotten what?"

"Never mind . . . Peter, does it have to be the mountains, isn't there any other way? You must have brought identification papers that would take you anywhere."

"Forged identity papers," he pointed out. "Nice authentic forged ones, yes. Four of them, actually, to cover a variety of people and intricacies of disguise and destinations."

She said earnestly, "Then why can't you and X leave the country an easier way? Those mountains, Peter—even if it is summer!"

"What easier way?" asked Peter. "Easier how? Think a

minute. We're more than three thousand miles from Peking right now, and not much closer than that to Canton. To head for either would mean train, bus, plane, hiking, and remember X and I won't be traveling as American tourists, we'll be natives, subject to checkpoints and queries. No, there are too many variables," he said with a shake of his head. "Too many bottlenecks, risks, and cliff-hangers, whereas the mountains are only six hundred miles away from where we are now. And besides," he added mischievously, "we just might meet the 'Mother-Queen of the West' somewhere in the Kunluns."

" 'Mother-Queen of the West?' "

He nodded. "There are surviving records of an adventurous emperor back in 600 B.C. who liked to go exploring. His name was Wa Tei and he went off traveling in the west with his retinue—a large one, I gather—and he's said to have penetrated as far as the Kunlun mountains that divide Tibet and Khotan. That's where he met the Mother-Queen of the West—a kind of Queen of Sheba person—who ruled this strange top-of-the-world land. He was lavishly entertained and brought back stories that have turned into myths and legends, rather like Homer's tales. Except," he added, with a smile, "a good many of Homer's stories were assumed to have been myths and turned out to be real. Who knows, it could happen to me!"

"A Shangri-la," breathed Mrs. Pollifax, her eyes shining. "How absolutely wonderful!"

"Of course," he added, "it may have been a scruffy little mountain village full of dirt and lice—"

"Don't," she begged. "I demand a Shangri-la."

"Mrs. Pollifax, you're a romantic."

"I know," she told him happily. "I am, I insist on it—but so are you, I think?"

"Guilty," he acknowledged with a boyish grin. "But legends aside, it's true that it may be more rugged skirting the Tarim Basin and the desert but we can travel by night on donkeys, avoid people almost entirely, and go at our own speed. And there *is* a British weather expedition somewhere in those mountains if we can find it."

"As well as the ghost of the Mother-Queen of the West." She nodded. "Of course as soon as you mentioned *that* I knew there wasn't a shred of hope that you'd change your mind. A British weather expedition sounds rather persuasive, too."

"If it can be found," he said politely.

"If it can be found," she agreed politely, and thought how unreal it was to be sitting here looking out on a dusty alley lined with sheds, tools, and carts and discussing with Peter a mere six-hundred-mile stroll toward mountain ranges that peaked at 28,000 feet. *I wish Cyrus were here*, she thought suddenly, and wondered if he was back in Connecticut yet; it was so very difficult to know, given those time changes crossing the Pacific; her logic in this area had never been trustworthy, and speaking of logic she wondered why she felt like crying whenever she remembered that Peter was going to die in three days . . .

Iris wandered out of the building looking distracted. "Oh dear," she said, sitting down beside them and pushing back her hair.

"Oh dear what?" asked Mrs. Pollifax.

"I don't know. I hope the free market comes next, I like the sound of it, I must be feeling very confined. What is it, by the way—have we been told?"

Peter said briskly, "Flirtation with capitalism. People in the communes are being allowed small parcels of land of their own now. Instead of selling their produce or pig to the government, they can sell it in the free market and keep the profit for themselves."

Iris' eyes opened wide. "But that *is* capitalism!"

Peter grinned. "It would be tactful not to use that word,

I think. Call it motivation instead. Actually *they* call it—''
He abruptly stopped, looking stricken.

He had nearly used a Chinese word, and Mrs. Pollifax
glanced quickly at Iris to see if she had noticed; she found
her staring into space without expression. A moment later the
others came out of the building and they climbed into the
minibus, and Peter gave Mrs. Pollifax a rueful apologetic
smile.

As he smiled at her Peter was thinking *My God that was
a close one, this is growing really difficult, I've begun to
think in Chinese and I almost spoke in Chinese in front of
Iris*. As he passed Mrs. Pollifax, already seated, she glanced
up; their eyes met and she winked at him.

He grinned, at once feeling better. *She's really something*,
he thought, taking a window seat two rows behind her in
the bus, and to his surprise he found himself wishing that
she could go with him tonight, when he planned to follow
the river to the labor camp. *She's getting to me*, he realized.
Me, the hard-line loner. He wondered what it was about
her that drew him, and for want of any cleverer insight
decided that it was a kind of capable innocence, but that
didn't fit either. There had begun to be a sense of kinship
between them; he felt at ease with her, which astonished
him.

At dinner Peter made a point of yawning a great deal,
which proved tiring in itself for there were twelve courses
through which to yawn. Because of their busy day there
were no plans for the evening, which was merciful, for an
early start mattered very much to him tonight. Jenny suggested a get-together in the small lounge for some singing,
a suggestion aimed at him, he realized, but he only yawned
and said he was going to catch up on his sleep.

Once in his room he quickly changed into the cheap
plastic sandals and gray cotton pants he'd purchased in

Xian, added a white undershirt and then—leaning over his canvas dufflebag—he divested it of the thin mountain-climbing rope with which he'd laced the bag. This he wound around his waist and chest before adding the khaki Mao jacket over the bulk to conceal it. Into pockets he thrust his jogging shoes and ID papers, and then brought out the very clever invention that tilted his eyes by ingeniously concealed tapes. Peering into the mirror at the effect, he grinned: he looked very much like the workers he'd seen all during the day. When he'd undergone his wilderness survival class they'd gone to great lengths to prevent him acquiring a tan; now he understood the thinking behind it because he'd seen very few dark Chinese. Both Mr. Li and Mr. Kan had complexions like bisque china, the skin very white and opaque. His own pallor, his heavy brows and slanted eyes certainly removed all resemblance to Peter Fox: he was Szu Chou now, as his papers proved.

Unhinging the screen at his open window he pushed it back, slipped outside, and became part of the night.

It was nearing midnight when he stumbled across the cave by accident. Only an hour earlier he had found the river, and in following it had left the road behind him, wading across at the only point where the stream narrowed. This brought him into difficult terrain where he had to use a flashlight. He disliked showing a light, but it appeared to be deserted countryside. Since leaving Urumchi only one truck had passed down the road—he had taken shelter in a hollow—and rather than stumble into trees and over rocks, wasting time he couldn't afford, he had to assume this area was equally as untenanted.

Half a mile after he'd forded the river the sound of rushing water grew thunderous, the river curved abruptly, and he met with a waterfall. Deprived of any means of crossing the river again he trained his light on the fall, judged it to be about thirty feet high, and stoically began climbing up the hill beside it, clinging to the roots of trees and to rocks and bushes. Once on the top he admitted—not without resistance—that a brief rest might be a good investment, a catnap would be even better, and he set his wristwatch's tiny alarm for thirty minutes. Finding a mossy patch among the rocks he sank down, leaned back, and promptly fell over. His assumptions had been wrong: the rock against which he thought he leaned did not exist; there were rocks to the right and to the left of him but he'd fallen into what appeared to be a cavity in the hillside.

Turning on his flashlight he parted the underbrush to examine what lay behind it, and his light picked out a hollow roughly twelve feet by eight, its ceiling a little over five feet, laced tightly with roots from the forest. In astonishment he stood up and trained his light on the ground above to see what had caused such a miracle. *Roots*, he decided: years ago a massive tree must have been struck down, leaving a space over which the surrounding root systems had slowly woven a carpet as they groped toward the support of the rocks on either side. On top of this network Nature had gradually deposited soil and moss, leaving the hollow untouched, and had then charmingly screened its entrance with underbrush.

There was suddenly no need for sleep. Excited, Peter checked his compass, crawled inside the cave, and sat looking around him in amazement. It was dry and warm inside. Bringing out his map he spent a few minutes computing his location, marked it in pencil and grinned: if his estimate was correct this cave was only a mile from the labor camp, and a perfect place to hide two people next week while the security police searched for X. It was better than perfect, it existed only ten feet from a rushing stream of water, and water was the most precious commodity of all.

Already in his mind he was making the commitment; now he backed it by groping in his pocket for the dried apricots and apples he'd brought with him for a snack tonight. These he deposited in the center of the cave, like a promise, and then he remembered the slab of chocolate from his previous nights' explorations, and added this to the fruit. With a glance at his watch he parted the underbrush and left, exhilarated by his discovery.

Continuing to follow the river upstream he arrived in a few minutes at a point where a second river joined with the first one to rush down toward the waterfall. From the pattern of it—the headwaters arranged like the crossbar of a T with the second stream dropping to waterfall and highway—he thought this had to be the river that led to the labor camp. Moments later he confirmed this when he shone his flashlight across the rushing water for a minute and its beam picked out piles of neatly stacked logs and cut trees waiting to be denuded of their branches. He had reached a logging area.

It was time now to find a way to cross the river and find the camp.

Peter began to reconnoiter, as yet paying no attention to the water racing past him but examining the trees on each bank, his flashlight twinkling on-off, on-off, like a firefly. Presently he found what he was looking for: a stout tree on his side of the river opposite several strong trees on the farther bank. Unwinding the rope from his waist he knotted it around the base of the tree next to him and knelt beside the river to study its currents. *Vicious*, he thought, *nasty and vicious*, exactly the sort of current that would sweep a man under before he had a chance to catch his breath. He sat down and removed his shoes and socks and hid them with his flashlight, compass, and papers under the tree. Then he tied the end of the rope around his waist and lowered himself into the water.

At once the rapids swept him away, the icy water knocking him as breathless as if he'd been given a blow to the solar plexus. The current tumbled him over and over, extracting what breath was left him while jagged rocks pummeled and bruised him. Only the rope saved him: considerably downstream it snapped him to a halt, threatening to cut him in half from the current bearing down on him, but it held and he was able to surface and breathe again. Now he began the fight to swim across the river, the rope holding him in place as he fought, struggled, dog-paddled, and at last fell across the opposite bank.

But the icy cold had invigorated him, and a moment later he was on his feet, slapping his arms and jogging-in-place to restore circulation. With the rope still around his waist he hiked back to the stand of trees opposite his starting point, and after untying wet knots with chilled fingers he secured the end of the rope around the base of the larger tree. Checking it he found just enough slack; the tree was well-rooted and the rope firmly engaged. When he finished it was still night but dawn was emerging almost imperceptibly from the darkness, the shapes in the clearing where he stood acquiring sharper edges: dawn was only an hour away. He was bone-chillingly cold and he was tired, but his reconnoitering was nearing an end, he would soon be on his run back to Urumchi with three days to complete his plans. He headed across the clearing for the shelter of standing trees where he suddenly stood very still, listening.

The rush of the water behind him was deadening to the ear but above it or below it he understood that he was sensing movement ahead of him. Human sounds: the murmur of voices, the shuffling of feet. Lowering himself to the ground he crept to the next stand of trees and came to a stop.

From his hiding place he looked out on a second clear-

ing into which a dozen or more men were marching in a
bedraggled fashion, dull shapes in a twilit world. Once in
the clearing they stood passively, a few wandering off to
lean against piles of wood, or to sit on logs while their
leader—or guard—gestured to men unseen as yet. Peter
saw the flare of a match; from the vaguely discerned
movements he deduced the men—prisoners—were smoking,
eating, or idly talking . . . a free moment before the day's
work began, a precious moment.

One of the men left the others and strolled toward the
cluster of trees behind which Peter hid. Quickly Peter
dropped to the ground again as the man paused beside a low
bush six feet away from him, fumbling at his trousers. He
was so near to Peter that he could see the neatly mended
patches in his drab shirt; from the ground he could peer up
and into the man's face and see him clearly.

And seeing him clearly he thought in a rush of shock,
But this man is Wang Shen!

He thought, *I haven't even found the labor camp and
here is X . . .*

He was shaken and incredulous. He didn't want it to be
X, some part of his shocked head insisted that it couldn't
be X, searched wildly for discrepancies, demanding doubt,
skepticism, second thoughts because this was not in his
scenario . . . And yet it *was* X, he had memorized that
face until he knew its very essence—the slant of the
cheekbones, the shape of the pointed jaw and the blunt
nose, the intelligent eyes, the rather sardonic mouth. This
was Wang Shen all right, and he was standing only six feet
away from him.

He thought, *Dear God, this is incredible—the cave and
now this.*

He thought, *It can't ever happen this way again. Not
like this.*

But he had no plans made yet, X was to be rescued

later, after he had divested himself of the tour group, he couldn't possibly do anything now, it was too soon, this was a mere reconnaissance. In only a few hours the tour group was to leave for Turfan, and it was already perilously close to the time when he must race back to the hotel. He couldn't afford any rescue attempt now, it would make him late and then they would all be in the soup, including—and most of all—Wang Shen.

"There's the cave," an inner voice reminded him.

"The cave *now?*" he protested. "Leave X there for two days when everything could go hideously wrong and I never get back to him? Abandon him there with only a handful of dried fruit, a chocolate bar, and no ID papers should something happen and I never reach him again?"

He thought abruptly, *I wish Mrs. Pollifax were here.*

The devoutness of that longing staggered him. He had believed he could manage everything himself and originally he had thought her preposterous, and now he wished above all else that she was here to advise him. "What would she say?" he asked himself, and then, desperately, "What would *she* do?"

Words suddenly came to him that she had used describing her meeting with Guo Musu. "Oh, I had no plans," she'd said to his amazement. "There comes a time when one has to trust oneself and whatever presents itself. It's like that occasionally."

Like that occasionally . . . of course. He was nearly exhausted, he was trembling with cold and he hadn't planned this at all, but he had found a cave and now he had found X. *My God,* he thought, *Mrs. Pollifax is more flexible than I am, and I'm twenty-two.* And with the memory of her words a sense of her presence returned to him and he grinned: Mrs. Pollifax would simply get on with the job, matter-of-factly.

And so—matter-of-factly—Peter proceeded to get on with the job: he softly called out Wang's name.

The man had just begun to turn away; he hesitated now, startled. Some distance away his companions were huddled over a tiny fire, their faces turned aside. Peter moved slightly away from the tree, just enough to expose his presence, and then quickly popped back. But Wang had seen him; his face had turned astonished and baffled. Peter extended one hand, thumb up. A moment later the man shuffled over to the tree and stood in front of it, curious but perplexed.

"You're Wong Shen," Peter said from behind the tree.

"Who—?"

"Also Wang Shen."

"*Zhe shi shenme?* What is this? Who are you? Where did you come from?"

"*Wo jiang* Peter—American, *Meiguo ren*—sent with papers to take you out of the country. Can you decide quickly? Are you well enough? To go *now?*"

"You're testing me," the man growled. "Long live the great and correct Communist Party of China!"

"*Ta ma de,*" swore Peter, "the time is *now.* I've a rope across the river, it can be done before there's too much daylight, there'll never be such a chance again."

"Why?" he asked harshly. "How is anyone interested in me?"

Peter said impatiently, "Because the Russians have learned who you are and they'll be after you next. *Lai bulai*—are you coming or aren't you?"

There was silence. Peter waited in suspense for the man's friends to call to him, or for Wang to call out to the group and betray him, and then abruptly, calmly, the man moved around the tree to peer at him and his glance was searching. He said, "You look very young, with good food in you."

"I hope I also look American—my eyelids are taped."

Studying Peter's face the man's gaze seemed to come from far away, as if he drew on a part of him buried very deep, and then his eyes sharpened, he returned to this cold misty dawn and to the moment. He said with infinite dryness, "If you have found me—if you have managed to cross that river—what have I to lose? Let's go!"

Thank God, thought Peter. Wang glanced back once at the clearing, bent over to look at a root, dropped to his knees and crept behind the tree, his movements without haste, measured, as if he had long ago learned the art of blending into backgrounds to avoid attention. Peter dropped to the ground with him and they crawled together to the next copse of trees; reaching it they stood up and raced to the stream.

"You can do this?" Peter asked X, pointing to the rope which the dawn was illuminating now.

Wang's thin frame shivered in the cold. "*Shi*," he said, and stepped forward. Testing the rope first—he seemed incredulous at its lightness—he lowered himself into the icy river. Hand over hand, at times almost submerged by the current, he propelled his body to the other side, climbed out, shook himself, and stood up. Quickly Peter untied the rope from the tree on his side—there must be no signs of their departure—and once again knotted it around his waist. This time he leaped far out into the water and was better able to control his entry into the rapids so that when the rope pulled him up short he was within a maneuverable distance of the opposite shore. A moment later he was out, and joining Wang upstream.

"We can talk later," he said, pulling on socks, buckling on his sandals and stowing flashlight, shoes, and compass into his Mao jacket. "And the faster we go the warmer we'll be," he added, trying to still the chattering of his teeth, "although I'll say right now that your escape was planned for next week, not today. We must be resourceful!"

The man gave him a sharp glance but said only, "Let's go then."

They reached the cave within the hour, losing only a few minutes searching for it. Pulling aside the branches concealing it Peter said, "This is the first miracle, Wang, the second was coming practically face to face with you when I was only reconnoitering."

Wang crept into the cave, amazed. "Truly this *is* a miracle."

"You're not so strong as you seemed at first," Peter said. "You couldn't run."

Wang's smile was kind. "We're given very little food."

Peter nodded. "And I've little to offer you—look."

Wang only shook his head. "What you have here—just to see fruit and chocolate—looks a feast to me. I am also expert by now"—his tone was humorous—"in foraging in the woods. What exactly is the situation?"

Briefly Peter explained it. By now he had begun doing rapid calculations for his own preservation, and he was worried and tried not to show it to Wang. It had taken him four hours to reach the cave, for instance, and it would take him at least another four hours to return to Urumchi . . . Already it was past four in the morning and breakfast for the tour group was to be served at 8 A.M., with a departure for Turfan at nine. He would be too late for breakfast and even his return by nine was now problematic: how he was to explain his absence was beyond his capabilities at the moment. He concluded his story to Wang by saying, "And so you must rest and grow stronger here, for the mountains. When the tour group returns from Turfan late tomorrow I'll bring you more food, but as you can see—"

Wang had sat down on the cave's floor and now he smiled for the first time. "Don't worry please, I will enjoy extremely this release from *jian ku lao dong*," he said, using the word for hard physical labor. "It is enough to be free. *Wo lei le*—I'm tired."

"Okay, but watch any tracks you leave in the woods when you go out," Peter counseled. "Remember, they'll be searching for you soon. When I return I'll whistle like this." He gave a soft bird call and repeated it twice. "Got it?"

Wang was looking happily around him. "Yes, yes," he said absently. "Some apricots first, I think, and then I will sleep. I may even sleep for days!"

Peter said, "Good. Only wish I could . . . *ziajian!*"

"*Ziajian*," responded Wang, but by this time Peter was already outside and beginning the long hike back to Urumchi, a trip made all the more conspicuous and hazardous by the growing light of day.

10

By SEVEN O'CLOCK THAT MORNING MRS. POLLIFAX HAD already guessed that Peter wasn't back—she had knocked early at his door, feeling obscurely troubled about him— and when they assembled in the lobby at eight for breakfast and Peter still didn't appear her worry sharpened and she prepared for the worst. They were to leave for Turfan in an hour, their luggage had already been collected and Peter's absence had become obvious and serious. The list of horrors that might have happened to him seemed endless to her: he could have been picked up by police as a local native for questioning; he could have been picked up as an American with fake ID papers; he could have met with an accident and be lying alone and helpless somewhere; he might have found the labor camp only to be discovered himself. Whatever had gone wrong he was not here, and he ought to be here.

The door to the dining hall opened, they walked in to breakfast and Mrs. Pollifax—feeling embarked on a roller-coaster ride whose end she couldn't foresee—sat down and without enthusiasm attacked a hard-boiled egg.

Mr. Kan, hurrying in, said, "I have knocked and he doesn't hear, the manager is to open the door with a key, he may be ill."

"Are *you* feeling okay?" Malcolm asked Mrs. Pollifax from across the table.

Jenny, seated next to her, turned and stared.

"Fine," said Mrs. Pollifax and gave them each a forced bright smile.

"Oh he'll turn up," said Iris cheerfully, earning a bland smile from Joe Forbes and an admiring one from George.

Mr. Li stuck his head through the door to call to Mr. Kan, "He's not in his room. He slept there but he's not there."

"Slept there," murmured Mrs. Pollifax: that meant bed turned down and sheets wrinkled . . . she was relieved to hear that Peter had thought of this, except of what use was a turned-down bed if Peter didn't reappear soon?

"But nobody has seen him," added Mr. Li, coming in to join them, and he did not laugh merrily; he looked anxious and puzzled.

"We don't leave for Turfan without him, do we?" asked Jenny.

The two guides launched an intense discussion in their own language until Mr. Li shook his head. "We must. The arrangements have been made. At nine we will notify security police, of course."

At nine o'clock when they filed out to the waiting bus, still speculating on Peter's absence, they were met by a sleek gray limousine pulling up in front of the hotel, a "shanghai car" as they were called, bearing white curtains at the windows to conceal its occupants. It looked very official and very menacing: *They've arrested Peter*, thought Mrs. Pollifax with a sinking heart. A gentleman in a soft gray Mao uniform climbed out of the car, followed by a smiling Peter.

"Hi," Peter called out cheerfully. "Sorry I'm late, everybody—went for an early morning jog and got lost until Mr. Sun rescued me. Very high official, speaks American!"

An early jog, thought Mrs. Pollifax, and her gaze moved to his outfit, the pants rolled to his knees, legs bared down to his running shoes, Mao jacket tied around his waist, and a T-shirt emblazoned with the words MOZART LIVES.

Beautiful, she thought, paying tribute to Peter's resourcefulness. Heaven only knew what he'd had to discard to present such a picture, but if one overlooked the absence of his ubiquitous blue jeans, he was the perfect jogger, face flushed, eyes bright, and even in China they must have heard of the American passion for jogging. She felt a leap of excitement, the very same feeling that overtook her at sight of one of her *pelargoniums* breaking through the earth: Peter, too, was blooming. He'd carried it off. Somehow. The tension had snapped; Mr. Sun was speaking benevolently to Mr. Li and Mr. Kan, who looked both pleased and honored, and Peter, giving Mrs. Pollifax a broad impish grin, dashed into the hotel to wash his face.

Several minutes later as he walked up the aisle of the bus he leaned over and whispered in Mrs. Pollifax's ear. "You *what?*" she gasped.

He nodded, grinning his triumph. "The job's done. Quite a night!"

"But how—what—"

"Later," he said. "Collect food, X will need it when we get back. Collect everything," he added and looked up as Iris and George walked down the aisle. Glancing at his watch he said, "Now I've got four hours to sleep—talk to you later." He continued to the rear of the bus and promptly stretched out across four seats. Jenny, following, looked affronted and abruptly sat down next to Joe Forbes.

X found . . . X already freed, thought Mrs. Pollifax in astonishment. What could have happened, and how could it have happened? What had taken place during this endless night?

The bus began to move—they were off to Turfan—and Mrs. Pollifax's thoughts moved with it: backward and then forward but no matter where they went they returned to the fact that Wang had been removed from the camp and hidden. How pleased Carstairs would be, she thought; how pleased *she* felt for Peter . . . suddenly it had been *done*, and she was smiling as she glanced out of the window at the hulk of an old bus they were passing, and then rough adobe houses with pale blue wooden doors.

"What does that sign say?" she heard George call to Mr. Li, pointing.

"It says, 'Protect our Motherland and Heighten Alertness,' " he called back.

As if to illustrate its message Mrs. Pollifax glanced up at a distant hill—they were leaving Urumchi behind now—and saw anti-aircraft guns silhouetted against the sky, and posts strung with barbed wire. *Against Russian invasion*, she reflected, *but it looks as if the Soviets won't find Wang now. He's ours.*

Now they were passing fields of yellow rapeseed, with clusters of commune huts in the distance. Off to their right the mountain range they followed had the shape and color of sand dunes, strange and surreal to the eye, and then the road straightened and was lined with poplar trees on either side, closing out the mountains. They began to meet trucks carrying laborers to the fields, but there was smaller traffic, too: handmade carts that hugged each side of the road and were put together out of wood with large old rubber tires for wheels, some pulled by one or two horses, some pulled by a man between the shafts. The poplars thinned and then vanished as they emerged into flat treeless country, and here Mrs. Pollifax became aware of the stone-lined irrigation trenches parallel to the road, with here and there women washing clothes in the water.

But having purred with satisfaction for a contented interval, Mrs. Pollifax's thoughts now approached certain new uncertainties, retreated from them, and then returned to face and examine them. It was all very well, she thought, to say that phase two had been triumphantly accomplished, but there was no getting around the fact that the rescue of Wang was to have been phase three, not phase two. X was tucked away now but with a long and dangerous wait ahead of him, and obviously with nothing to eat or Peter wouldn't have mentioned collecting food; and what if—perish the thought—Peter could never return to rescue him? *As soon as I see Peter alone*, she decided, *he must tell me where the cave is. Both of us should know . . . and in the meantime we must pray that he's not discovered by the Sepos.*

Her eyes went back to the land, to a long flat lovely valley they were crossing, the mountains a marvelous pastel blue in the distance. Far away her gaze picked out a walled clay compound, dusty beige against the dusty beige of the earth. The mountains drew closer here to them, incredibly wrinkled like very old faces, and then—suddenly —in the midst of nowhere they came upon a factory with nothing in sight but piles of slag, the sky, the road, and the distant mountains.

Such space, thought Mrs. Pollifax, *such enormous tawny space. But why a factory here, and how does anything arrive or be taken away?*

Her thoughts returned to Peter's message in the bus. She could collect food for X, yes, lining her purse with that plastic bag she carried and slipping food into it at the table, but this meant that Peter would have to make still another trip out into the night when they returned to Urumchi. This meant no rest for him; how long could he go without a decent night's sleep, she wondered, and still think clearly for what lay ahead?

Across the aisle Jenny was growing restive. "Let's wake him up," she told Joe Forbes in a loud voice directed at Peter in the rear. "He's slept long enough, don't you think? Hey Peter!"

"He looks very comfortable," pointed out Joe Forbes, smiling.

"But he went to bed early last night, right after dinner," Jenny said, pouting, "and jogging can't take that much out of anyone!"

Mrs. Pollifax turned and said politely, "I'm not sure that he went to his room to sleep last evening, he mentioned letters and cards to write."

Clearly Jenny didn't welcome this intrusion; she looked startled, mumbled, "Oh well," and subsided. It occurred to Mrs. Pollifax that it had been clever of Peter to use Jenny as cover during the early days of the tour, but his choice was showing signs of boomeranging. Jenny looked ready to cry again; she was not going to take his defection graciously. *A strange girl*, she thought, and wondered what caused this penchant for overreacting.

On either side of the road the country was flat and empty, with the consistency of gravel, but there were surprises: a sudden glimpse of rail tracks, of freight cars on the dusty horizon being loaded with crushed stone, and then of workers strolling along the road wearing dust masks, and then—abruptly—a huge body of water in the middle of this arid dead land, fed by runoffs from the mountains and dropped like a shimmering blue jewel into the warm dry panorama.

In midmorning they stopped beside a shallow irrigation stream and Mr. Li produced Lucky Kolas for them. After this they were off again through the Koko Valley to begin their descent into the Turfan depression, crossing an interminable valley of gray slag, the only signs of civilization the crisscrossing railroad and power lines. At times it gave the illusion of being a gray beach stretching toward a gray sunless sea in the distance.

"Very prehistoric," Malcolm said, leaving his seat to join her. "I hope by now you're a trifle bored with your thoughts, as I am with mine. Feel like talking?"

She smiled. "Yes there's a time for thinking and a time for talking." *And a time to stop worrying*, she added silently.

He said easily, "I find I can all too easily succumb to group mentality; it has a nice cozy hypnotic quality, rather sheeplike and very comfortable."

"Are you feeling refueled now, after being quiet?"

"Definitely. I don't feel that you're a group person, even if you do function well in one. George Westrum, for instance, is a group person totally, mainly because he lacks any original thoughts to entertain himself while alone."

Mrs. Pollifax gave him an amused look. "Rather hard on him, aren't you?"

Malcolm said simply, "He has been instructing Iris in the butchering of his steers and how they are sent to market, with side excursions into profit and loss. He sits behind me, I can't help overhearing. I doubt he's noticed an inch of the country we've been passing through."

"And where is Joe Forbes on your scale of ten?" she inquired.

He smiled. "Not the loner I first thought him to be. There's that need to please, and to smile all the time, plus that lamentable determination to practice Chinese on the guides and to ingratiate himself. I think in general he might be called an Ingratiator.''

Mrs. Pollifax, finding his pithy comments almost as interesting as Cyrus' might have been, asked, "And Iris?''

He brushed this query aside impatiently. "Iris is simply Iris.''

"Meaning what?''

He smiled, his quizzical brows drawing together. "Why, an original, pure and simple. A transformer and a transcender.''

"You like her then," said Mrs. Pollifax. "Or appreciate her. Yet give every evidence of avoiding her.''

He grinned. "I avoid George, to be blunt about it, and since he's in constant attendance on Iris, well—there it is.''

"And Jenny?''

Malcolm stopped smiling. "A rather troubled person, don't you think? The trip seems to be putting her under enormous pressures. Nice little thing, a pity. I have the feeling—''

"Psychically or intuitively?" intervened Mrs. Pollifax humorously.

"Pressure," he said, ignoring this, "can go either way, it creates diamonds, it also creates explosions. What are your feelings on the matter?''

"At the moment—given her tears the other night—I think explosions.''

"Followed, one hopes, by clearing skies," he said. "At the moment she seems extremely cross about Peter having a nap. Do I see green up ahead?" he asked. "Yes, a rather dusty green but definitely green. Do you think we're approaching Turfan?''

This seemed possible because Mr. Kan was unwinding his microphone and presently standing up to explain Turfan

to them: a city with a population of 120,000, containing
seventy farms and where, for about thirty days of the year,
the temperature lingered at 113° F., and in winter descended
to twenty below zero . . . Its irrigation system was unique,
consisting of underground tunnels, some of them two thousand years old, through which the runoff from the distant
mountains reached this desert city . . . And this afternoon
they would be introduced to this underground system.
Whereupon he promptly sat down.

"Short but to the point," said Malcolm, "and since the
air conditioning's just been turned on it's doubtless 113°
Fahrenheit right now."

"I see we're back to red clay," mused Mrs. Pollifax,
looking out of the window. "My goodness, I just saw a
field of cotton."

Soon she was seeing grapevines, too, and mysterious
greenery growing behind the walls of compounds, but here
there were wooden bars set into the clay windows, and
large wooden gates in the walls that showed the Turkish
influence Peter had mentioned. On this road it was small
tractors that pulled the wooden carts; presently they passed
a traffic jam of army trucks, and then a bazaar shaded by
squares of canvas and surrounded by parked donkey carts
and bicycles. "And here we are," announced Mr. Li as
they swung down a broad dirt road and turned left into a
large compound of whitewashed walls. "The Friendship
Guesthouse. Lunch in one hour!"

A square hot room with cement floor and walls; two
narrow beds and a window; a huge round fan whirring at
top speed on the bureau; a bathroom with a shower tap, a
dripping faucet, and no tub or stall . . . Mrs. Pollifax went
to her door and called after the others, "Anyone want to
walk to that bazaar down the road before lunch?"

Iris poked her head out from the door of the room next to hers. "I take it your room's as hot as mine? Count me in!"

Jenny said defiantly, "Joe and I are going to sit in that grape arbor and check our cameras."

But Peter said, "I'd love a walk!"

Once in the bazaar Mrs. Pollifax bought recklessly for X: several ripe golden melons, tiny apricots, raisins, nuts, and a string bag in which to carry them, and for herself a pair of cloth shoes and a kerchief. She was about to add some grapes to the collection when she abruptly felt giddy and close to fainting. The heat, she decided, a strange kind of heat because the sun was only moderately bright. She looked at the man from whom she had bought raisins: he sat solidly under a strip of canvas wearing a white skullcap, his face shaded. Something in her eyes must have explained her dilemma because he jumped up, grasped her arm, and sat her down on his box in the shade of the canvas.

She smiled gratefully. He offered her water but she shook her head, remembering that it wouldn't be boiled. Across the pathway from her she saw Peter talking to a young native who appeared to be enthusiastically practicing his English; George Westrum was taking a picture of the rows of rubber-tired carts that had been turned into selling stalls with the addition of canopies, boards, and boxes; Iris had crossed the irrigation trench and was trying to approach a water buffalo that had wandered into the scene. Mrs. Pollifax's sympathetic friend was still offering her water with a mounting insistence. Making no impression upon her he pulled off his skullcap and pantomimed the pouring of water over it and into it.

"Ah!" she cried, understanding, and brought out the kerchief she'd just purchased. He nodded eagerly and she held it out to him while he poured water over it; she placed it on her head, delighted by its coolness, and thanked the man profusely with gestures.

"That bad, huh," said Peter, joining her. "Look, I want you to meet my friend over there, he speaks a little English and I've got a deal going with him that includes you. In fact it seems to *depend* on you."

"On me!" she exclaimed, and as the sun struck her again she recoiled. "Peter—"

But he was already saying to the young man, "Sheng Ti, here is my grandmother."

Mrs. Pollifax gave Peter a reproachful glance. "Not *another* grandmother, Peter?"

"Ah yes," cried Sheng Ti, bowing and smiling, and she looked at him with interest.

His face was at variance with his clothes, which were disreputable: neatly patched pants, a sweat-stained dirty undershirt, and sandals repaired with string; his face, however, shone with intelligence, and his eyes were bright and eager.

"Now that you see my grandmother you will do this for us?" Peter asked him. "To win the bet—the wager?"

"Bet, yes. For the lady yes, I understand now," he said, nodding vigorously.

"Okay, then. Outside the Guesthouse. Wait down the street at the corner, okay? Very secret. Ten o'clock tonight." Peter counted out change and placed it in the young man's palm. "Ten o'clock, Sheng Ti," he added, holding up all of his fingers.

"Ten," repeated Sheng Ti.

As Peter led her away Mrs. Pollifax glanced back and said, "Peter, what on earth—what was all that about?"

"He wouldn't do it for me," Peter told her, "so I tried him out on you and it worked. An authority figure, that's you," he said, grinning. "I think he's what's called a 'hooligan'—no visible means of employment so I took a chance on him, he ought to be relatively safe.''

"Safe for what? Peter, you didn't speak Chinese to him!"

"God no," he said. "I'm just a crazy American tourist wanting to win a bet, a bet that I could drive a donkey cart for a couple of hours without the guides hearing about it. I had a hunch he might be open to something illicit. We'll need to hide our foodstuff and sheepskins in the desert, and how else could we get them there? Besides, you're not used to missing all the fun, are you?"

She laughed.

"Disguises later, after we leave Sheng Ti behind tonight," he went on. "A kerchief for you, that quilted jacket you bought in Urumchi—"

"Very observant of you," she said dryly.

"—cotton slacks, and I'll slant your eyes for you after we've left Sheng Ti, in case we're stopped." He signaled to an ancient man with a seamed face sitting patiently over his cart and donkey. "Hop on, he's a cab driver, Turfan style, and you've got to get out of this sun."

She gratefully pulled herself onto the shelflike rear of the cart, smiled at the driver, and waved good-bye to Peter, thinking how confident and thoughtful he was becoming—and also quite dear, she added, startled by this realization. How unbelievable this would have seemed to her in Hong Kong and Canton, or even in Xian when he was being irresponsible and hostile, and with this there came a strange feeling, not unfamiliar to her, that all of this had been intended to happen, and that her meeting with Peter held a significance that was not apparent to her yet. She was delivered to the entrance of the Guesthouse, gave the driver a handful of *feng*, and returned to face the heat of her room, passing Jenny and Forbes seated talking under the luxurious grape arbor. She felt only a little giddy as

she examined her treasures from the bazaar and put them
away but when she left her room for lunch and sightseeing
she wore a dripping wet towel wound around her head.
She did not plan to nearly faint again under Turfan's sun,
and if her day had just been extended by a cart ride into
the country with Peter, it would at least be cooler by night.

There were no keys to the rooms here, so that when
Peter knocked softly on her door at ten that night he
followed this by quickly slipping inside. Speaking in a low
voice he said, "We can leave by your window." He was
carrying his dufflebag and he placed it now on her bed.
"What do you have?" he asked.

"A second padded quilted jacket from Xian," she told
him crisply. "In Urumchi I bought two sheepskin vests,
one small blanket, and of course, there are the vitamins
and dried foods I carried with me. And to fit all this into
my suitcase," she reminded him, "I had to leave almost
everything behind in Urumchi except my pajamas. Even,"
she added sternly, "my hairbrush."

"I'll lend you mine," he said dryly. "How are you
carrying it all?"

"Rolled up in a bundle." She pointed to it sitting on the
floor beside the chair.

"And may one ask what's happened to your two lower
front teeth?" he asked with interest.

"Ah," she remarked happily, "that was a dental bridge.
I noticed an old lady in the bazaar this morning with
missing teeth, and I thought it would add an authentic note
to my disguise." She knotted the plain cotton kerchief
around her head, patted her cotton jacket and leaned over
to adjust the buckles on her cloth shoes. "Shall we go?"

Peter unlatched the screen, removed it, helped her over
the sill and followed, replacing the screen behind them. In
single file they stole up the path in the darkness, passing

the lighted rooms of the others and coming to a stop at a certain place in the wall where the top had crumbled, releasing the pointed shards of glass embedded in its cement to repel intruders. Tossing both dufflebag and bundle over the wall, they were soon outside the compound and moving toward the street's corner.

The cart was waiting with Sheng Ti beside it. A fuzzy moon dimly illuminated his features; he gave them and their luggage a glance that unsettled Mrs. Pollifax by its thoughtful speculations. He said, "I go with you?"

Peter smiled and shook his head. "No, we'll be okay. Back in two hours."

"I did not steal it," Sheng added, his eyes running curiously over Mrs. Pollifax's cloth shoes, pants, and quilted jacket.

"Good," Peter said and tossed their baggage into the rear, handed Mrs. Pollifax up to the seat with a flourish and squeezed in beside her.

Sheng Ti handed him the reins. *"Zaijian,"* he said, and stepped back into the shadow of the wall.

The donkey moved, the cart lurched, the wheels gave one outraged groan and they were underway; when Mrs. Pollifax glanced back Sheng Ti had vanished. A lone cyclist pedaled toward them in the darkness and called out a greeting; Peter returned it, slipping easily and gratefully into Chinese. "But I think we stop now and make our eyes slant before we run into anyone else," he said, and pulled up beside a vacant stretch of wall.

"What a peculiar contraption," said Mrs. Pollifax when he shone his flashlight once and very quickly, after inserting it under her hair.

"The amazing thing is that it doesn't hurt and it can't be seen—and now you are a true Han," he told her, and she saw the flash of his smile in the faint moonlight.

Slowly they proceeded down the road and out of Turfan,

occasionally meeting cyclists as they returned from work
or pedaled to work, the pale moon etching black shadows
of walls and trees across the darkness of the road. A dog
barked. A voice was heard from behind a wall. Other than
the clip-clop of the donkey's hoofs and the movement of
the wheels there was only the silence of the desert around
them.

"How absolutely beautiful to be free for a couple of
hours!" said Peter with a happy sigh.

Since Mrs. Pollifax was already experiencing this same
reaction—a sense of elation at being out and into the space
around her and free of Mr. Li, Mr. Kan, and the tour
group—she said with feeling, "Pure bliss! It's safe to
speak English now?"

He gestured around them at the empty pale countryside.
"Who's to hear?"

And so they began to talk. Of families. Of what they
had left behind to come to China. Of the desert. "The
Taklamakan desert," Peter told her, "has been called a
hungry and ravenous monster. It's considered far more
treacherous than the Gobi, it eats people and cities, swal-
lowing them whole."

"*Cities?*" she said incredulously.

He nodded. "Entire cities that flourished in the days of
the Silk Road. They find them now and then, the archaeologists, and there are probably more treasures buried there
still than you or I could ever imagine, as well as the bones
of men and animals caught in its violent dust and earth
storms."

She shivered. "We're not on the desert yet, are we?"

"No, and won't be. Only its rim."

"And you and X—you won't cross it, will you?"

"No—skirt it."

As they talked, their voices low in keeping with the

rhythm of the plodding donkey and the clouded moon binding them in its spell, she thought and spoke of Cyrus.

"Why don't you marry him?" asked Peter bluntly.

"If we get out of it—if I get out of this in one piece, I intend to," she announced with a firmness that startled her. "It seems to me now that I hesitated—oh, for all the wrong reasons. Foolish ones."

"Someone said that if the heart is engaged—"

"Yes," she said, nodding. "And mine is. I hesitated, wanting to be sure, feeling—oh feeling that life would be different, changed, if I married, and that I might have to give up—all this."

"All this," murmured Peter, and suddenly smiled. "So you're an adventurer, too!"

"Yes—no—yes, of course I am," she admitted, laughing. "But what I overlooked—"

"Yes?" he asked curiously.

"What I overlooked," she said simply, "is *change* . . . Meeting Carstairs and becoming useful to him changed me so that nothing was or ever could be the same again." *Like a kaleidoscope*, she thought, remembering that simile following her first adventure. "But meeting Cyrus also changed me so that nothing will or can be the same ever again. *Nothing*. Not even this," she added ruefully. "Which is what I didn't see clearly until now."

"You're not sorry you came?" he asked.

She shook her head. "Oh no! There were things I had to learn, as you can see. Important things. Even at my age!"

He said with a sigh, "I think my parents stopped learning a long time ago, which made me a misfit, a changeling, and restless. A very conventional middle-class family, except they did send me to Harvard where I didn't belong either but—"

"But where you learned to speak Chinese."

"Yes. Funny, isn't it? It came so easily to me, without

any classes or lessons at all, as if I'd spoken and read it before and it was already etched in my subconscious waiting to be rediscovered. You must know the very Eastern theory that we've lived many lives; can you believe in that at all?''

"Easily," she said, nodding. "For a long time I've found it a very supportive, meaningful explanation for the curious things that happen to people: the tragedies, the uncanny rescues, and coincidences in life." She laughed suddenly. "And Cyrus has a rather mandarin look about him; he's a large man and very American, but there's an oriental cast to his eyes that drew me from the beginning. Just as I've been drawn to the country of China itself," she added meditatively.

"Think we've known each other before?" asked Peter, with a chuckle.

She thought without saying it aloud: *yes it's possible, why else do I feel so connected with you—suddenly and inexplicably—and so alarmed about what lies ahead for you? There's an understanding between us, unspoken but familiar, that I've experienced only with Tsanko and with Cyrus.* Aloud she said quietly, "It's quite possible, yes. A sense of fatefulness—of stars crossing—happens rather frequently to me these days. I lived a very prosaic life, you see, and then suddenly I too met Carstairs, and I've often wondered if this strange new life was waiting for me all the time during those years I lived so quietly. I've wondered," she added softly, "how much choice we really do have about some of the large events in our lives. Is Peter Fox your real name?" she asked abruptly.

He shook his head. "Peter's my name but not Fox." He glanced down at his luminous digital watch and said, "We've been in transit exactly fifty-five minutes, I think it's time we stop and look for a place to hide all this gear."

She looked around her at the low, hunchbacked surrealistic mountains off to their left. They had to be sandstone, she thought, to have been whipped into such frenzied, angry shapes by wind and rain, and to have created the gulleys and earth cleavages among which they were riding now. "It's certainly a good place to hide things, but however will you find your cache again?"

"By compass, by noting distance and direction of travel, and by making a map of the shapes and contours. C'mon," he said, bringing the cart to a halt. "I really need your help, we've only a few minutes to do this. *You* pick the place. Take the flashlight."

Mrs. Pollifax said sharply, "No, Peter, no flashlight."

Startled he asked, "Why?"

"I don't know." She stepped down from the cart, gave the donkey an absent pat on its flank and moved off the road toward three jagged rocks about six feet high. "I think here," she called.

Peter was already lifting out his dufflebag. She went back and retrieved her own bulky package and when she joined Peter she could see him nod in the dim light. "Good," he said, and bringing out his knife he worked away at enlarging a hole under one of the rock formations. Into this he pressed the small items: vitamins, melons, two filled water pouches, the dried fruit, and the socks, finally sealing the gap with a stone. On the surface between two of the rocks he laid out the bulkier items—the two pairs of boots and the sweaters—and then covered them over with the sheepskins and at last the rug. With his knife he scraped enough dust from the earth to scatter over the rug until it looked a part of the earth.

"Not bad," commented Mrs. Pollifax. "But let's not linger. *Please*."

He gave her a sharp glance, found several loose stones

to weigh down the rug and nodded. "Okay, let's go. We'll both pace off the distance to the road, okay?"

They each found it to be fifty-two feet.

"You drive while I make notes," he told her, handing her the reins. "Or at least what notes I can manage without a light. I don't understand you, why not a light?"

"Not yet—later, but not here," she told him, surprised by the depth of her unease. With some difficulty she turned the donkey around on the road and they began their return into town. She noticed that Peter worked over his notes like an artist, glancing up, holding out his arm to measure and to squint, writing and drawing sketches into his notebook until at last he lighted a match inside cupped hands and checked his compass. "I hope you're not implying that someone's been watching us," he said.

To cover the strange flash of alarm that she'd experienced she said lightly, "Let's just say I'd hate to see you and X reach that cache and find nothing. You'll be coming to it from where?"

"*Not* from Turfan," he said and pointed over his shoulder. "We'll start out from the cave in the mountains and head southwest, bypassing Turfan, and after rescuing our sheepskins we'll move south toward the Bagrach Kol, or Lake Bosten," he explained. "Then we'll roughly follow the oases towns along the desert, keeping at a distance from them, naturally."

"Yes," she said, and was silent, feeling her dread for both him and X.

They returned to Turfan, driving down the same broad road, the cart intruding only lightly on the deep silence of the night. When they reached the corner of the Guesthouse wall Sheng Ti appeared suddenly out of the shadows, advanced toward them, put a finger to his lips counseling silence, and spoke directly to Peter in a low voice.

It needed a moment for Mrs. Pollifax to realize that

Sheng Ti was speaking to Peter in Chinese. She said in alarm, "What is this? Why does he speak to you in—"

"He heard me greet that damn cyclist in Chinese," Peter said grimly, and swore. "What is it, Sheng, what's the matter?"

Sheng no longer troubled to speak English, he was obviously agitated, his voice breathless, his gestures quick.

Peter turned to look at Mrs. Pollifax. "How did you know?"

"Know what?"

"Sheng says we were followed on foot by someone from the Guesthouse. Very stealthily, very secretly. And seeing this he followed that person, whoever it was, and thus trailed *all* of us into the desert."

11

Aᴛ ᴛʜᴇ ʀᴀᴍɪꜰɪᴄᴀᴛɪᴏɴꜱ ᴏꜰ ᴡʜᴀᴛ Sʜᴇɴɢ ʜᴀᴅ ꜱᴀɪᴅ Mʀꜱ.
Pollifax gasped, "One of the guides?"

Peter turned back to Sheng. "No—no, Sheng says *not* a
native, he is sure of this. He says this person wore some
kind of cloak, so it could have been a man, it could have
been a woman—I asked him—but he is certain it was a
foreigner, very definitely, because of the way this person
walked and acted."

She drew in her breath sharply, remembering her searched
suitcase and realizing that it had never been far from her
mind. *Something is wrong,* she thought. *Terribly wrong.*

She accepted Sheng's judgment, acknowledging his
shrewdness and his street wisdom. "Where is this person
now?" she asked.

"Back in the Guesthouse."

She turned her attention to Sheng Ti, realizing that he must be dealt with first of all. "What does he think or suspect about all this?" she asked. "Does he perhaps expect money to not speak of this to anyone?"

Peter spoke to Sheng in Chinese. "He says he wishes to talk with us alone somewhere about why we carry baggage out of the city and return without it. He feels that he alone saw the baggage we carried—which is probably reassuring if I ever find time to think about it. He also wishes to know why I concealed my speaking Chinese so well, and why suddenly you have two teeth missing and dress like a Chinese woman."

"Yes," she said. "Where can we talk?" But she was thinking, *Someone in this tour group knows about Peter and me. Someone among them knows why we're here. How could this have happened? Who else would know about Wang? Who else would even be interested in Wang?*

"Not far," Peter was saying. "You think we can trust Sheng?"

"For the moment I think we have no choice," she said dryly, but in examining her initial reactions to Sheng she added, "I believe we can trust him, yes, but in any case I have a brown belt in karate."

Peter laughed. "Wouldn't you know! Okay—he says we leave the cart and walk."

She thought, *There is no one—absolutely no one—who could know about Wang or be interested in him.*

Except the Russians, she remembered in horror.

Carstairs had said, "One of our agents who works for the Soviets—a double-agent, needless to say—has brought us information of X's existence and of the Soviets' interest in him."

Had brought them information on X's existence . . .

Information that came solely from the Russians, who

badly wanted Wang for themselves . . . The same Russians who supposedly had plans to abduct Wang later in the summer . . .

Supposedly . . .

But what if instead, knowing themselves persona non grata in China, they chose to leak their information to the CIA and let the Americans find Wang for them instead? Let an American agent enter China and find the labor camp, find and release Wang and then . . . and then . . . *Oh God*, she thought in horror, *could Peter and I be walking into a trap?*

They were following Sheng through narrow alleys, turning left and then right; he stopped now beside an abandoned irrigation ditch spanned by a crumbling bridge. Sheng led them under the bridge and gestured to them to sit down.

Peter said in surprise, "He says he sleeps here, this is his home."

They squatted, knees touching. Sheng had been eating garlic which made for a powerful atmosphere; he was also anxious, and this too contributed an odor so that they hunched together in a cloud of garlic, sweat, and dusty earth. "But why is this his home?" asked Mrs. Pollifax. "Why doesn't he have a unit like everyone else?"

Peter began to speak to Sheng, and Sheng replied at length, and while they talked Mrs. Pollifax's mind flew back to Carstairs' mysterious counteragent. If all the information came from the Russians and they were being followed . . . She shivered a little, exploring the idea of herself and Peter being mere pawns because if her theory was correct and if the Russians were masterminding this operation, then it would be a member of the KGB who had been planted in the tour group.

To watch them. To snatch Wang for the Soviets once he was free.

And Carstairs doesn't know, she thought, trembling at

the prospects should her suspicions be right. *He doesn't even guess and there's no way to communicate, to tell him that possibly . . . maybe . . .*

Peter turned to her and said, "He tells me that he's twenty-six years old and he's *hei jen*—it translates as being one of the 'black persons,' living without registration and without a ration card or employment. He lives off friends or steals and sells things in the black market."

"Good heavens," she murmured with a glance at Sheng.

"He says that you and I must have very good identification papers to have dared to go out tonight dressed as natives. He wants either my ID papers or yours. He says he can pay. He wants to use them to escape to Hong Kong."

Mrs. Pollifax considered this with interest. "So he won't betray us then," she said with some relief. "Not if he wants something from us." The word *betray* struck her forcibly and she thought, *Carstairs has in effect been betrayed by his double-agent, his counterspy, hasn't he? and doesn't know this either.* Aloud she said, "But how did he come to live under a bridge and be *hei jen?* He looks very intelligent, I'm curious."

She had to wait again for the reply, watching Peter's gestures and the changes in expression on his face as he listened: surprise, thoughtfulness, a frown, a nod, until at last he resumed. "He says it began for him with *shang-shan xia-xiang*—what they call 'up to the mountains and down to the villages' . . . the many young people sent down to the country to learn hard physical labor. Sheng was *cheng-fen bu hao*—bad background, meaning his family used to be rich peasants, landlords. Because of this he had no hope of school or a job in the city. He was sent to a commune in central China where the farmers hated these city youngsters foisted on them . . . this was ten years ago, when he was sixteen; he felt lonely and ostracized. He stood it for three years and then he ran away. For this he was given *shou-liu*—detention—and then he was sent to a commune near Urumchi where they work on the roads. Here he acquired more bad records—*tan*, or a dossier. What it amounts to—to sum up—is that he couldn't conform."

"I'm not sure I could have either," commented Mrs. Pollifax thoughtfully. "But how on earth does he survive?"

Peter said in a level voice, "He steals. People sometimes give him food. Once he stole a cartload of melons and set up a stall in the bazaar and sold them. With the profits he bought pumpkin seeds and nuts and sold them, and then jars of honey . . ."

"Sounds a promising businessman," said Mrs. Pollifax, giving him a smile.

"He saved up money for a Flying Pigeon bicycle—one of the best—but being without a unit and without coupons he had to go to the black market to buy it. The man took his money but never produced the bicycle and since then he says his anger has given him much despair, he sleeps too much and has gone back to stealing."

Mrs. Pollifax said impulsively, "But there's such sensitivity in his face, and look at those eyes. He shouldn't be an outcast."

Peter said, "I've told him his country is changing now that Mao's dead, and that mistakes of the past are being corrected. If he just waits a little longer—"

"What does he say to that?"

"He asks how these changes can reach him. They are very slow, and even slower this far away from Peking. He says he has nobody to speak for him, nobody to say he is not bad, he says he is now an invisible person." Peter shook his head. "We could never sell ID papers to someone like him, not with his background, he's not reliable."

Mrs. Pollifax looked at Sheng, an idea occurring to her

that she liked very much. He returned her glance, a sudden flash of anger illuminating those black eyes. "I do not beg," he said, thrusting out his jaw.

"If you should leave your country," she asked him gently, "what would you do, what would you want?"

He scowled at her. "To go to school. To work."

She nodded and turned back to Peter. "Well?"

"What do you mean 'well'?" he said indignantly. "As I just said, with a background like that he's scarcely reliable, he'd blow it. He'd be picked up and he'd blow the whole thing."

"Not if he left the country with you and Wang," she told him.

"If he *what?*"

She said slowly, "It's true there would be three of you if he joined you, and three are harder to hide in the countryside, but he's a master of hiding, isn't he?" *And if there is danger ahead*, she added silently, *three can fight better than two.*

Peter grinned. "Hearing you cracks me up, it really does."

She conveniently ignored this. "In the mountains you'll need help with X, who may not have your stamina. Sheng could turn out to be valuable to you, and how can he 'blow it,' as you say, if he's with you all the time? Frankly I feel he'd be extremely reliable if it helps him to get out of the country."

Sheng was looking at her intently; she could feel his tension as he comprehended what she was saying; she could hear the quickening of his breathing, as if he waited with an incredulous hope.

"You'd trust him?" Peter said.

"Yes," she said simply.

Sheng sat very still; it was as if he'd not heard her but very slowly she saw his shoulders straighten, and when he lifted his head it was to say with dignity, as one equal to another, "*Xiexie*. Thank you." And then to Peter, "You sell me papers? I may go?"

Peter was silent and then he nodded. "Okay. But I give you papers, not sell them, and you go with me. To the south and over the high mountains." He translated this into Chinese.

When Sheng understood what Peter was saying he visibly trembled with emotion. Impulsively Mrs. Pollifax reached out and touched his hand and saw the gleam of a smile: it was the first time she'd seen him smile, and it was a smile of incredulous joy. He said fervently, "I will not fail you, I can die for this."

"It will be very hard going," Peter reminded him.

She said gently, "Peter—"

"Yes?"

"He knows what hardship is. He can somehow make his way to Urumchi, can't he? Give him papers and money and have him meet you somewhere near the hotel there."

"Yes," Peter said dazedly. "You don't think he'll—?"

"It's a good way to find out, isn't it?" She stood up. "Peter, I want to go back now, I feel very uneasy about our being followed. I want to think—to see—to check—"

He looked startled. "Oh—yes, of course," he said, and then, "I ought to be thinking about that, too."

Very tactfully she said, "I'll think about it now, you can think about it later." It had needed all of her will power to concentrate on Sheng Ti and his situation when instead she had wanted to cry out to Peter, *If what I think is true then someone in our tour group is here to find Wang, too. They've known who you are from the beginning and they've searched suitcases until they identified me as your cover because they knew just what to look for and they found it in mine: that preposterous hoard of dried foods and vitamins. Peter, don't you see what this means?*

In silence Peter and Sheng escorted her back to the compound and around the wall to the corner where they had scaled it earlier; she was boosted over it to creep stealthily to her window, where she removed the screen and climbed back into her room, securing the window behind her. For a moment she stood in the darkness, her mind checking and rechecking the thoughts that had dazed her during the last forty-five minutes, but her conclusion remained the same: someone in their tour group could be working for the Russians, and she and Peter could be in grave danger.

Hearing a faint sound beyond her door she tiptoed across the room and quickly opened it just in time to see a shadowy figure pause by the door next to hers, open it, enter and close it softly.

But that was Iris' room, she remembered, and she thought, "Iris?" and then in astonishment, *"Iris?"*

By the luminous dial on her bedside clock it was half-past one in the morning but Mrs. Pollifax did not feel like sleeping. She sat in the darkness for a long time, not enjoying her thoughts or speculations at all.

M<small>RS. POLLIFAX AWOKE WITH A START TO DISCOVER THAT</small>
both heat and daylight had arrived and that she had
fallen asleep across her bed, still in the costume of the
previous night. The huge electric fan was wheezing from
exhaustion. Walking into the bathroom to wash her face
she was confronted by a mirror over the washbasin that
reflected a strange slant-eyed woman; she hastily disen-
gaged the tape hidden under her hair and watched Emily
Pollifax emerge again. The sense of pending heat was
oppressive; she felt vaguely worried still, and jaded from
those worries; she had not slept well. She stood on the
slatted shower platform while a thin stream of lukewarm
water poured over her, and she wondered what Cyrus was
doing now. At this exact moment. He seemed very far away.

Having dressed in her thinnest and coolest clothes she walked out to the grape arbor to sit down and face her day. Putting her head back she gazed into the tightly laced green leaves above her and at the clusters of pale green seedless grapes grown in Turfan, Mr. Li had said, for fifteen hundred years. Presently a door in the long line of rooms opened and Malcolm emerged, glanced around, and strolled over to join her.

"I scarcely recognize you without a wet towel around your head," he said dryly.

"After breakfast," she promised him.

He nodded. "Breakfast in that incredibly hot little room with two fans, one of which doesn't work, and George Westrum manages to find the only place where the working fan stirs any air."

"Courage," she told him, "it's only half-past seven. Except—where is everyone?"

Two doors opened simultaneously: George Westrum emerged from his and Iris from hers; they smiled, greeted each other and walked together toward them. Jenny came next, followed by Joe Forbes, and then Peter hurried out looking surprisingly fresh and bright eyed. They sat or sprawled under the grapes, their conversation desultory and idle as they waited for Mr. Li.

He joined them looking both serious and somewhat anxious, so that their greetings did not extract from him his usual beaming smile.

"What's up for today?" asked Forbes.

Mr. Li nodded. "We spend most of today in Turfan, of course. This morning we visit the Thousand-Buddha Caves, also an ancient tomb, and following lunch we look forward to Jiaohe—ancient city—and then return to Urumchi." He hesitated and then turned to look at Peter. "You were not in your room last night, Mr. Fox."

Mrs. Pollifax's heart skipped a beat. *Oh dear*, she thought in dismay.

"I beg your pardon," Peter said coldly.

"You were not in your room all night," Mr. Li repeated firmly.

"And how the hell would you know that?" asked Peter, rallying, while the others listened in astonishment.

"Because I looked in—there are no keys, as you know. I looked in and went back many times to look. You were not in your room all night."

Mrs. Pollifax thought, *I've got to stop this; I've got to think of something* . . .

"I don't know what business it is of yours," Peter told him.

"It is the business of myself and China Travel Bureau," he said formally. "I am responsible. You were not in your room, you were not anywhere in this compound. I have to ask, *where did you go?*"

They had all frozen into a tableau staring mesmerized at Peter, who stared back at Mr. Li; they had been made uncomfortable by some unknown quality in Mr. Li's voice, and by the rising suspense of a long silence that Iris broke at last by speaking.

"Actually," said Iris in a calm voice, "Peter spent the night with me. In my room. All night."

Every head swiveled toward Iris, and George Westrum gasped. Mrs. Pollifax looked quickly at Iris and then her glance moved to George who was staring incredulously at Iris, his mouth open; she saw that his face had turned white, as if he'd been struck. *How strange this is*, thought Mrs. Pollifax, *all of us simply sitting here and watching*.

Peter said, "Iris—"

"It's quite true," she said with a lift of her jaw. "He was with me."

George leaned forward, his eyes cold with anger and

disgust. "You *slut*," he said, biting the words through his teeth and he rose to his feet and stalked out of the arbor, his back rigid.

His words seemed to reverberate, or was it the hate behind them, wondered Mrs. Pollifax—oh those tight thin lips, she thought, this had been there all the time. Even Mr. Li looked stricken. In an embarrassed voice he said to Peter, "If that is—I didn't—"

Malcolm said pleasantly, "Surely it's time for breakfast now, don't you think?" He stood and walked across the arbor to stand casually behind Iris' chair, and Mrs. Pollifax loved him for this. Iris herself sat very still, a flush on either cheekbone, her head high.

"Yes indeed," said Joe Forbes, as if coming out of a trance, and jumped to his feet.

Iris looked around, her face without expression, her glance resting lightly on Mrs. Pollifax, and then she too stood up.

Jenny, staring at her, said, "Well of all the—!"

Mrs. Pollifax heard herself say firmly, "I think we've had enough."

Jenny gave her a hostile glare and turned to Joe Forbes. "*Poor* George," she said dramatically.

"Poor *Jenny*," he said lightly. It was the first evidence that he'd given of being aware of the shifting alliances.

They moved across the compound in procession, Malcolm walking silently beside Iris, Joe Forbes and Jenny with Mr. Li. Peter, falling in at the rear with Mrs. Pollifax, said in a low voice, "I'm in shock."

"Accept, accept," she murmured.

"But—why did she do it?"

"I don't know," she told him. "I just don't know, Peter, but it's becoming terribly important that we talk in private soon. I think there could be more shocks ahead. Where's Sheng Ti now?"

"On his way by bus to Urumchi, I hope. I suppose you mean you're worried about what Sheng told us—that we were followed last night into the desert?"

"Yes."

He said with a frown. "You realize we have only Sheng's word for that, don't you? You and I haven't seen anyone, we have no proof. He could have made it up to hide the fact that he followed us himself."

"Possibly," she conceded.

"But in any case," he added, his face lightening, "tomorrow's the day for visiting the Kazakhs up in the grasslands, and at some point during the day I expect to vanish, which will take care of anybody's lurking curiosity." With this confident statement he held the screen door open for her to enter the dining room.

This time George did not capture the enviable spot in front of the one working fan; he did not join them at all for breakfast.

Mrs. Pollifax, with dampened towel wrapped around her head, forced herself to concentrate on sight-seeing for the next hours. There was nothing else to do, she decided: she was experiencing a sense of events moving inexorably now toward their conclusion and without any way to alter or color them. That word *inexorable* again, she thought with a shiver. X was hiding in his cave at the edge of the Tian Shan mountains, while Sheng Ti was somehow making his way to Urumchi, armed with his coveted ID papers at last; they too would head for Urumchi again toward the end of the day, and Peter had reminded her that in only thirty or so more hours he planned to disappear. In the meantime they had been mysteriously followed into the desert last night—she did not share Peter's skepticism about Sheng's tale—and Mr. Li had known Peter was gone. If one of the members of the tour group had told Mr. Li of Peter's absence, she could no longer believe that it was Iris. Iris had provided cover for Peter at a rather staggering cost.

Sticks and stones may break my bones, she thought, reflecting on that cost to Iris . . . *a good name is rather to be chosen than great riches* . . . Why had Iris leaped to protect Peter? What did she know, and how? She discovered as they embarked on their sight-seeing that she was carefully avoiding Iris, going to great lengths to neither walk with her, speak to her, nor catch her eye, and then to her chagrin she noticed that Iris was going out of her way to avoid her, too. It was as if each of them knew something about the other they didn't care to acknowledge, but what *had* Iris been doing outside her room at one o'clock in the morning?

Since there was no answer available to her—because she wasn't even sure just now of the question—Mrs. Pollifax philosophically gave herself up to the moment, and to their excursion into the desert to see the Thousand-Buddha Caves. This was not at all difficult: they had arrived at the heart of the Silk Road and it was an incredible countryside, totally emptied of colors to which the eyes were accustomed. It was a land of beige—beige, terra-cotta, cream, tan, and dusty gray, set into a valley of surrealistic shapes: harsh angles cut into sandstone cliffs, mesas pleated and wrinkled by wind and sun, and jagged tawny mountains climbing in tiers to a heat-seared washed-out sky. Nothing moved, nothing appeared to live except the shapes, which had a life of their own.

Yet it felt neither unfriendly nor desolate. The sense of space was glorious, and the palette of earth colors were as warm as if they'd been toasted by the nearly-suffocating sun. Leaving the bus for the caves Mrs. Pollifax looked down in astonishment on an oasis of bright green, long and narrow like a knife-slit between the jagged sandstone hills, a miraculous ribbon of green threaded by a canal carrying sparkling water down from the mountains. Standing on the cliff overlooking this oasis Mrs. Pollifax was transfixed. In her mind's eye she saw a long line of camels, horses, donkeys slowly moving up this trackless valley to arrive at this oasis with its glacier-fed running water, so incongruous in the midst of the heat and sun and desert. In her imagination she could hear the tinkle of camel bells and voices calling to one another in the exotic languages of the Silk Road. If they were leaving China, they would be heading for Persia, India, Russian Turkestan, the camels laden with silk, furs, ceramics, jade, iron, lacquer, and bronze; if entering China they would be bringing gold and precious stones, asbestos and glass, wool and linens, and— perhaps most significant of all—the religion of Buddhism.

"Yes," she whispered, "this is *it*, this is what I came to see, what I hoped to feel." And she stood lost in the magic of it until Mr. Li's call to her broke the spell.

They lunched back at Turfan in the small hot room with its malfunctioning fans, with George again seizing the one promising spot for air, Mrs. Pollifax's returning cheerfulness was not altogether shared by the others, however; subtly they had now formed themselves into two camps. Although there was not the slightest acknowledgment of it by gesture, glance, or word, Mrs. Pollifax and Malcolm had tacitly united to protect Iris, and Peter along with her. The others, thought Mrs. Pollifax dryly, were being far more obvious in their allegiances, and in the case of Jenny even strident. Jenny had come into her own: she now had George and Joe Forbes in attendance, and although her voice was shrill all of her elfin charm had returned. Like a Lady Bountiful she offered everyone the raisins she'd bought in the bazaar the day before, not even affronted when Mrs. Pollifax and Peter refused them. George's baseball cap had taken on a more cocky angle, but his face remained a mask of tight-lipped coldness: he seethed with anger. Joe Forbes appeared to observe Jenny as if she were a precocious child, but Mrs. Pollifax thought that he was enjoying very much being in the center of things for a change.

After lunch they were off again to see the ruins of the city of Jiaohe, but they were growing accustomed now to the desert, to its tawny shades of cream and beige, to the far horizons and to the hints of Turkish influence as they passed through Turfan: the boots, the occasional sash around the waist, the kerchiefs worn around the head by the women, the higher slant of cheekbones, and rounder eyes.

"The city of Jiaohe," explained Mr. Kan, taking up the small hand microphone in the bus and looking very serious, "was once the location of the royal court of Che-shi. It is sixteen hundred years old, having flourished in the year A.D. 200. This was very important communication center on the ancient Silk Road. Of such strategy—and importance, too, as you will see by its locale."

"What do you mean by that?" asked Jenny.

"It is built on steep cliff with ravines all around."

"What happened to it?" asked Malcolm.

"It was destroyed by roving bands in fourteenth century."

"Roving bands?"

"Muslims. Genghis Khan maybe. Nobody knows. It *died*." He snapped his fingers and smiled.

"More ruins," sniffed George, looking very warm and flushed from the heat.

"Looks like some sort of dried-up maze," Joe Forbes said, as they swung past the solitary caretaker's house and headed up the dusty road to the top of a broad mesa.

"But a child's maze," said Iris eagerly, her head craned to look. "People lived where, Mr. Kan?"

"You will see," he told her. "In small rooms—oh very dark, very small—inside walls."

The bus came to a stop, the doors opened, and they met

with desert heat again. Iris at once strolled off with Mr. Kan, who talked earnestly to her, delighted by her questions and her interest, but Mrs. Pollifax wondered if Iris didn't attach herself to him to avoid the others. Peter lingered to ask directions of Mr. Li, and George and Jenny moved off together. It was Malcolm who caught up with Mrs. Pollifax as they approached the walls that opened into a vista of lanes and alleys.

"Hot," she said, turning to smile at him.

"Very. Your towel dried out already?"

"I've timed it," she said. "It turns damp inside of ten minutes and dry in half an hour. Yes, it's now dry. You've been very thoughtful about Iris, by the way."

"Not at all," said Malcolm calmly. "I have plans for Iris—I intend to marry her, except I do rather hope she won't go around being so quixotic in the future."

Mrs. Pollifax beamed at him appreciatively. "Malcolm, you're wonderful," she told him. "I'm truly happy to have met you and I feel that I shall forever love your talking mice. You and Iris are a marvelously improbable combination, but now that I think of it terribly *right*. You wouldn't insist she stop falling over chairs or that she cut her hair?"

He smiled. "What, and lose that awkward flash of hands every few minutes? Not on your life."

"When did you decide all this?" she asked.

"Well, there's that psychic bit," he explained. "I had a nearly overwhelming reaction to her when I first saw her, which—as you may remember—was as she popped out from under a table in Hong Kong. I felt as if I'd been hit over the head, frankly. It took some time to understand what had happened, but there it was. . . . In any case I found her so funny, earnest, and unique that it scarcely needed any help from the psyche, although it's been very pleasant knowing all this time—really *knowing*—that she wasn't going to marry George, no matter how ardent he proved to be."

"But what about Iris and *Peter*?" she suggested mischievously.

He laughed and steered her to the left, down a slope toward a more intricate arrangement of walls. "Surely you know *that* was a lot of hogwash."

"George didn't," she reminded him.

"Well, George is a nerd, of course. He has excellent taste in women, but obviously he goes after form rather than content or he'd never have believed Iris for an instant. He has a small mind."

"Have you mentioned any of this to Iris?" she inquired.

"Good Lord no," he said, looking appalled. "Not being psychic she couldn't possibly know what I do. On the other hand," he added with a chuckle, "we have avoided each other assiduously for a week—suspiciously so—and I do hope I don't sound macho if I say there has been an intense awareness between us."

"I have been—not unaware," she told him, remembering the electricity she'd felt between them in Xian, at the tombs. "You're being very tactful, then."

"Oh, no, just giving her time," he said, and suddenly stopped.

"What is it?" asked Mrs. Pollifax, alarmed by the look on his face.

He had become immobile, his head turned as if to listen to something she couldn't hear. He said, "I heard—thought I heard—"

She said sharply, "Malcolm, are you all right?"

"Yes," he said. "Yes, yes—let's keep walking."

"What did you hear?"

He shook his head. His face had paled, he looked strained, but seeing her concern he managed a smile. "I'm fine, honestly. No problem."

Mrs. Pollifax was already fumbling in her purse for the smelling salts she carried with her. "No problem except that frankly you look awful. Here." She held out the small vial to him.

He grasped both her arms and the smelling salts and propelled her into an open space. "Look at all the shards lying around," he pointed out. "An archaeologist's delight."

"And note the signs in English suggesting no one remove any. Malcolm, what's wrong?"

He placed both hands over his ears. "I'm trying, I'm trying, except that covering my ears doesn't help, I can still hear them." He reached for her smelling salts and unscrewed the cap. "This won't help either," he said fiercely. "I still hear them. Voices wailing in despair, the same lamentations I felt—heard—at Auschwitz, except here there are no screams, just unbearable despair. Something very sad happened here," he said, looking around them at the sun-baked empty mesa.

"I wonder what," she said, her gaze following his, believing him, believing that what he heard was something lingering here from the past.

"Not violence—that's the strange thing," he said. "Just weeping and wailing, lamentations, and a terrible sadness."

"Malcolm let's get out of here," she told him. "You do look horrid, you know."

Peter, following down the path and coming upon them said, "What is it, something wrong?"

"Malcolm."

Peter stared. "My God he looks absolutely wiped out."

They helped him to his feet and slowly retraced their route back to the bus. As soon as they left the walls behind them Malcolm straightened and lifted his head, the color returning to his face. "It's okay, I feel better now," he told them both.

"The heat," Peter said, nodding. "I'll go and tell Mr.

Kan that it's bothering you. Sit and take deep breaths.''
He hurried off to look for the guide, filled with an energy
that defied the heat and promised well for his desert travels,
thought Mrs. Pollifax as she turned back to Malcolm.

"I always thought it must be quite fascinating to be
psychic," she told him. "An added dimension to life, you
might say. Now I see that it has its hazards and its price."

He gave her a twisted smile. "Hell sometimes. Sorry
about this, you won't mention it to anyone?"

"You notice I didn't," she said dryly.

"Good of you not to assume I'd gone off my rocker.
Hearing voices is one of the first signs, they tell me."

"You seem surprisingly sane to me," she said firmly,
thinking that if he should be their KGB agent, he was at
least a sane one. "When it happens in a ruin that's six
thousand years old . . . Auschwitz, too?"

He nodded unhappily. "They had to carry me out. Most
humiliating experience in my life. On a stretcher."

"Let's talk of something else," she announced. "I
think we should. Iris, for instance? Or the heat? Or—"
She suddenly wondered if he sensed or "saw" anything
about her, or about Peter, and for just a moment felt
endangered and uneasy.

The moment passed. Mr. Li, hurrying toward them in
the heat, called out, "I have sent Mr. Kan to find all our
people, the young lady Jenny is very sick."

Mrs. Pollifax sighed. "And a four-hour trip back to
Urumchi ahead of us? As group leader, Mr. Li, I do think
we must *go*."

Both Iris and Mr. Kan appeared from among the walls
supporting a very white-faced Jenny between them.
"Cramps," Iris explained, and accepted Mrs. Pollifax's
smelling salts. Jenny was installed in the bus on the rear
seat and a paper bag produced for her. Joe Forbes and
George Westrum strolled in from a different corner of the

city with Peter herding them like a shepherd rounding up a
flock. The bus started, and Mrs. Pollifax took one last
look at Jiaohe dreaming in the hot golden sun in its
sadness. *What did happen to you,* she asked silently, and
knew that she would always wonder.

Once again as they entered Urumchi they passed the
anti-aircraft guns silhouetted on the hills outside the city,
and the huge sign PROTECT OUR MOTHERLAND, HEIGHTEN
ALERTNESS. Threading their way through the sprawling
town they passed several factories belching sinister yellow
vapors, and then as they approached the wooded driveway
leading to their hotel Mrs. Pollifax looked from her window and saw Sheng Ti.

He was sitting by the road at the entrance, watching the
oncoming bus with great interest. She saw his intelligent
eyes focus on Peter, and then on her, and she quietly lifted
one hand to him, and smiled. Somehow he had made his
way to Urumchi. He was here.

The bus turned into the drive and Mrs. Pollifax, taking
stock, found herself grateful, and almost happy. Sheng Ti
had arrived to join Peter. They were back in Urumchi, and
it was gratifying to realize that she no longer need wear a
wet towel wrapped around her head and look like a beserk
Arab. She was bearing leftover food from their meals in
Turfan, all of it conscientiously, if wetly, stuffed into her
suitcase, and behind her in the bus Jenny had fallen asleep
at last after being actively ill a number of times.

But most of all, she thought as she looked back on
Turfan, she knew that she would not easily forget her trip
into the desert with Peter. They both carried back with
them the ramifications of that night—the knowledge that
someone had been watching them—but for herself she
knew that she would never forget that sense of leaving
time behind them for a few hours, of moving effortlessly,

slowly, into another century. It had diminished barriers and touched them both so that perhaps the closeness she'd shared with Peter was the most important part of the memory, and what had moved her most of all.

And because of this she decided not to tell him of her suspicions, not to burden him with them yet. They drew up to the hotel, and it was Mr. Kan and Mr. Li who went to the back of the bus to look after Jenny. Mrs. Pollifax, leaving the bus with Peter, whispered to him, "You saw Sheng Ti on the street out there?"

"I sure did." He nodded. "I'm really pleased. He made it."

"Do you go off with food for X tonight?"

He nodded.

She had to say it. "You'll be terribly sure you're not followed?"

"You can bet on it," he told her grimly.

"Good. What about your plans for the grasslands, for zero hour tomorrow?" she asked, and discovered that the word *tomorrow* chilled her.

He turned and looked at her as they gained the lobby, and she saw that his eyes were distant and cold, as opaque as they had been when she first met him in Hong Kong. He said curtly, "I don't think that you ought to know."

She didn't take this as a rebuff, she merely nodded, understanding the need in him now to withdraw and to build up that lonely austere strength that was familiar to her from her own experience. One couldn't share, not in this business, not with other lives at stake, and perhaps, she reflected, it was this experience of altered selfness that was the meaning behind all of her own adventures: a sense of bringing to each moment every strength and resource hidden inside of herself as well as the discovery of new ones: a sense of life being so stripped to its essence that trivia and inconsequentials fell away. It was very akin to a mystical experience, as she had realized long ago.

And so she only nodded. There would be no more sharing unless Peter found that he could afford it; Turfan was behind them, they were agents, and Peter the cold professional that she would never be. With equal crispness she said, "Right—just let me know if there's anything I can do."

He stopped and looked at her. "There's one thing you can do, yes. With your experience in people, you trust Sheng Ti? Really trust him?"

She said simply, "Yes."

Peter nodded. "Then I'll take him with me tonight to the cave and let him hide there with X."

"Very good," she said. "And I'll leave my contribution of food for them in your room when I go to dinner."

Due to their long drive back from Turfan it was a late dinner that evening, and for Mrs. Pollifax it was made even later by Mr. Li detaining her in the lobby as the others walked into the dining room.

He said, "There is this matter of Iris Damson and Peter Fox last night. As group leader, Mrs. Pollifax—"

"Yes?" she said without expression.

"It is most uncomfortable, and as group leader—"

"It *was* uncomfortable, wasn't it," she agreed, and remembering that the best defense was an offense she asked with great innocence, "However did you come to learn that Peter wasn't in his room? Who was it who told you?"

A curtain immediately dropped over Mr. Li's shiny black young eyes, and Mrs. Pollifax realized that she was experiencing oriental inscrutability; it did exist after all. She remembered that in Chinese society it wasn't the individual that mattered but the people. As group leader

Mr. Li would expect frank information from her, he would assume her proprietary interest in the group as a mass while certainly not giving anything in return. He said again, stubbornly, "As group leader—"

She smiled at him. "As group leader, Mr. Li, I insist we go in for dinner. Believe me, I'll do everything in my power to make things less uncomfortable for you, but on an empty stomach, no."

He looked suitably young and chagrined at this subtle reprimand for detaining her, but she also sensed in him an iron determination to probe and to bring order because this was his group, his tour, his responsibility. He was troubled by the implications of that confrontation in the grape arbor—*as I am, too*, she thought, entering the dining hall and taking her seat with the others, *but not for the same reasons*. The dinner had already begun. She grasped a spicy dumpling with her chopsticks and looked around the table at the others, studying each one carefully, seeing them all as likable, explainable, good people and to all appearances precisely what they seemed to be and said they were.

As I am too, she thought with a rueful smile.

There was Malcolm, so debonair with his guardsman's moustache and quizzical brows, his talking mice, and his psychic talent: she disliked very much the thought that he might be dissembling, but he could very well be the cleverest of them all. Her glance moved to Joe Forbes, bearded, smiling and affable; she had met her share of college professors with that same innate blandness of personality, as if the world of academics stifled contact with the outside world and preserved them in aspic. And there was Iris . . . Iris had already proven herself a remarkably good actress when she had lied for Peter, but her rescue of Peter could just as easily be a diversionary tactic, a deliberate attempt to confuse and disarm, for after all Iris *had* been up and abroad that night, the only member of the group to be seen, and her knowledge of Peter's absence had been made obvious. She turned her gaze to George Westrum, tight-lipped and flushed, half-boy, half-man in his baseball cap; if he wore a mask it was surely to hide the truculent child that he'd so brutally unleashed at Iris in Turfan. And then of course there was Jenny with her bright smile and tart tongue, missing from the table tonight and presumed to be asleep.

When the soup arrived to complete their meal Mrs. Pollifax excused herself, wanting very much to be alone. She told herself that following the heat, dust, and tension of Turfan the only thing that mattered at the moment was the gleaming white bathtub in her room. She did not want to speculate any longer on who had followed them into the desert, she wanted to forget and to rest, except that deep down she knew that what really caused her malaise was the knowledge that tomorrow night, if Peter was successful, he would not be with them anymore.

Zero hour.

At breakfast the next morning a very wan Jenny came to the table to sip a cup of tea; Malcolm's experience at Jiaohe appeared to have left him tired; George Westrum merely played with his food, eating almost nothing. Only Iris and Joe Forbes and Peter ate heartily, but Mrs. Pollifax thought that in general the group was approaching a nadir, as perhaps groups had to when moved about with increasing speed, without a free day to assimilate.

She herself had slept well, but on waking, and realizing that this was Thursday and grasslands day, her appetite had completely vanished. They were to spend the day in the mountains, with a picnic at midday, and under ordinary circumstances this would have sounded delightful.

Today, however, was not an ordinary circumstance. She

ate three roasted peanuts, nibbled at a hard-boiled egg, and then excused herself. Peter, following her down the hall, caught up with her and said in a low voice, "You were right, Sheng's really okay."

"He's with X?"

He nodded. "They hit it off right away—a pair of bloody nonconformists, those two."

She said quickly, "Peter—"

"Mmmm?"

She stopped to face him, wanting him to know much more than she dared to say to him in words just now. "Peter, listen and hear me, it's important. *No matter how successful today proves to be, don't relax your guard. Be careful!*"

He said impatiently, "Of course I'll be careful."

She shook her head. "You don't understand, Peter, I don't mean just careful, I mean you must expect—I don't know what—but assume—" She hesitated. "Assume that something could be wrong, very wrong."

The amused skepticism in his eyes died away in the face of her urgency. "All right," he said quietly. "I'll accept that, I'm hearing you."

"Good luck," she told him and entered her room, realizing that her major fear now was that Peter's sleight-of-hand, whatever it might be, might backfire and there be a corpse after all: Peter's.

"Let go," she told herself. "This is his problem, not yours. *Let go . . .*"

Once again they climbed into the minibus following breakfast, but this time they headed for the mountains surrounding Urumchi, climbing slowly, exchanging terracotta and dust for the green of spruce and fir trees. They passed a Red Army barracks, and Mrs. Pollifax wondered if this could be the one that Guo Musu had checked on their map; if so they must be quite near the labor camp from which X had been so surprisingly removed already. They turned right, stopping at a checkpoint—a hut from which a man emerged to examine Mr. Li's credentials—and then they headed up the narrow dirt road, passing a scattering of yurts on the hillside, surrounded by browsing sheep and goats. Already the air had become cooler, and Mrs. Pollifax drew on a sweater. The meadows grew more and more tilted and the trees moved in closer until after several miles of climbing the forest hugged the road. The bus slowed, they passed a shadowy glen lined with picnic tables and then came out upon a wild and forbidding area dominated by a waterfall.

Why it felt so forbidding Mrs. Pollifax didn't know, but certainly it did not strike her as hospitable. The waterfall was spectacular, as high as a three-story building, and its water fell like a silver curtain to the rocks below, making all the appropriate sounds, but there was no sun here, the mountain rose steeply on the left, like a wall, and the narrow paths cut out of the earth held puddles of water from the fall, and looked slippery and dangerous.

Mr. Li, showing it to them proudly, said, "This is where we picnic after the horsemanship of the Kazakhs. We stop to leave the beer here in the mountain stream to cool it for you." Mr. Kan was already unloading cartons from the bus and carrying them one by one toward the water.

"Will they be safe?" asked Jenny.

Mr. Li laughed. "Oh yes! On weekends there are many students here from the university, but today, no." He added as an afterthought, "Very dangerous walking here, the rocks extremely slippery. Only two weeks ago a student fell from above and was killed."

Mrs. Pollifax's gaze sharpened and she glanced quickly at Peter. She thought, *This is where it will happen, then, this is where Peter disappears. A shoe, a jacket left behind,* some indication of a fall . . . Peter was staring intently at the rocks and at the rushing water, his eyes narrowed, his face expressionless.

"But for now," said Mr. Li, gesturing them back into the bus, "the show of horsemanship please. Too early for lunch!"

Herded into the bus they set out again, and soon met with open space that slowly widened and broadened until they drove up and into a breathtaking expanse of green meadowland that stretched as far as the eye could see, lined on either side by mountain ridges. Mrs. Pollifax felt at once a sense of relief to see the sky again, and the sun. She heard Malcolm say, "This resembles Switzerland—it's amazing!"

Perhaps, yes, thought Mrs. Pollifax, except that several yurts occupied this end of the long stretch of meadow, and the faces of the men approaching the bus were swarthy and high-cheekboned and they wore blue Mao jackets and scuffed boots. Mr. Li conferred with them, announced that the demonstration would begin very shortly, pointed to elevated areas along the meadow, and suggested that they stroll there and wait.

"Stroll and wait," repeated Iris, grinning as she jumped down from the bus. "Have we been doing anything but?"

"Travel fatigue," suggested Malcolm sympathetically. "We'll all get our so-called second wind in a day or two and be off and running."

"Well, that will beat strolling and waiting," teased Iris.

Mrs. Pollifax said nothing; the picnic area and the waterfall had added a sense of oppression to the anxiety with which she'd begun her day, and she felt that her entire being had given itself over to waiting, waiting for Peter to engineer his disappearance. *I must stop watching him*, she thought, and seeing how cheerful he looked she felt almost cross with him. They reached one of the more inviting knolls and sat or sprawled on the grass while off to their right, in the distance, the Kazakhs began to group with their horses, talking and laughing among themselves.

"It looks terribly macho," said Iris suspiciously, watching them.

Joe Forbes had brought out a pair of binoculars and was peering through them. "Two of them are women, though," he told her, "and hooray, they're going to begin now."

The demonstration began, and proved so superb that Mrs. Pollifax almost forgot about Peter for the next half an hour: the Kazakhs galloped down the meadow to show off their splendid mounts, then held several good-natured races, followed by a game of tug-of-war over the pelt of a sheep. This, explained Mr. Li, had in older days been tug-of-war over a live sheep, but this they were spared.

"Terrific horses," Peter said. "Wouldn't mind trying one of them myself." It was the first time Mrs. Pollifax had heard him speak since they'd left Urumchi.

"Oh could we?" breathed Iris eagerly. "I've ridden all my *life*!"

Mr. Li looked shocked. "Oh—impossible," he said flatly.

Iris said, "The show's over, do let's try! Mr. Li, come along and translate for us, okay?"

Mrs. Pollifax lagged behind as the others surged down the slope to meet with the Kazakhs; she was beginning to feel bored and restless, which she knew to be the result of her rising suspense: since she found suspense difficult to deal with she simply wanted this day to be gotten through as straightforwardly and quickly as possible, and to see it interrupted by this distraction rather annoyed her. It seemed pointless and tedious, but of course she and horses had never enjoyed a warm or comfortable relationship. By the time she joined the group in the meadow she saw that Mr. Li's translating, and Iris and Peter's eagerness, had produced an effect: Peter was being allowed to mount one of the horses, a Kazakh holding on to the bridle. Cautiously the horse and Peter were led up and down the meadow and then with a laugh and a shout the Kazakh released them both and Peter effortlessly, joyously, cantered back to them on his own.

They all cheered his performance and the Kazakhs, huddled and watching, grinned their approval.

"Terrific!" shouted Iris. "Me next?"

"How about me?" asked Forbes.

Peter, still mounted, grinned down at Mrs. Pollifax. "Somebody give *her* a horse," he told them. "Group leader and all that. C'mon, we'll all take your picture, Mrs. Pollifax, what d'ye say? Ask for a horse for her, Mr. Li."

Mrs. Pollifax, laughing, shook her head. "No thanks!"

"Try," said Malcolm, as a horse was led over to her. "You can show your grandchildren the picture and—"

"Just sit on it," Peter told her. "C'mon, be a sport."

Mrs. Pollifax winced, recalling certain past incidents with horses and then decided to swallow her reluctance and opt for the role of Good Sport. Both Malcolm and Forbes boosted her into the saddle and there she sat, very stiffly, with Peter on his horse beside her and holding the reins for her.

"See? You've done it," he told her. "Not bad, is it? Take her picture fast!" he called to Malcolm.

He leaned over and adjusted something on the saddle of Mrs. Pollifax's horse, except that whatever adjustment he made did not appear to please her horse. It snorted, reared in alarm and took off—there was no other word for it, her horse took off like a jet plane in ascension—so fast there was neither time for Mrs. Pollifax to breathe or to scream, the problem of survival being immediate and consuming as she struggled to stay mounted on this huge creature gone mad.

Down the length of the meadow they flew, she and the horse joined together by only the most fleeting of contact: Mrs. Pollifax hanging on in desperation, each thundering jolt an assault on her spine, her hands groping for the elusive reins, for the horse's mane, then for his neck, for any accessory available as an anchor to keep her from being tossed into the air and then to the ground. Behind her she heard shouts, Peter's voice, and almost at once the sound of Peter on horseback in pursuit. The words he shouted were unintelligible, blotted out by the pounding of horse's hoofs.

Mrs. Pollifax prayed: that she would not fall off the horse . . . that she *would* fall off, but gently . . . that Peter would reach her quickly and bring her to a halt. But the horror of it was that the horse had only one direction now in which to go, and that was straight ahead and *up*—up the steep and wooded ridge ahead of them—and—"Oh God," she prayed as the horse raced in among the trees and without faltering began to climb, so that instead of crouching near his neck she was suddenly sliding backward now, her hands clutching his mane, which—she thought wildly—was scarcely a way to soothe or to appease him. Up they went at a 90-degree angle, the crazed horse slowing a little but not, felt Mrs. Pollifax, from any change in his determination to destroy her, and certainly not from repentance, but due entirely to the steepness of the hillside.

Now, she thought as he slowed—*now* is the time to jump. To fall off.

It was at this moment of resolution that she discovered her right foot was entangled in a stirrup. She shook her foot impatiently but it refused to be freed; she dared not look down at her foot, it felt irrevocably captured, and then the moment of possibility had passed, they arrived at the top of the ridge and Mrs. Pollifax caught a fleeting glimpse of what lay ahead and abandoned all hope.

What lay ahead was *down* . . . down through forest to miles and miles of flat desert intercepted only by one deep slice cut out of the earth—a small canyon, too broad to cross—and inside of her she screamed. Screamed for Cyrus, for Peter, for some magical hope that was beyond her. She saw her life pass in front of her, prepared herself to relinquish it, and in one giddy moment foresaw their end. Down the ridge they plunged at breakneck speed, Mrs. Pollifax thrown forward again, fighting to keep from sliding in and under the horse's neck, her foot still entangled. They reached the bottom of the mountain and the horse's hoofs struck the hard flat surface of the desert. Lifting her eyes Mrs. Pollifax looked ahead and saw now that the deep cut in the earth contained a boiling racing mountain stream and that the horse was going to leap that canyon and that he was not going to make it. Nor would she.

And all because she had mounted a horse to have her picture taken . . .

In one last desperate frenzy Mrs. Pollifax applied herself to disentanglement. Hanging on recklessly by one hand to the horse's mane she slid her other hand down to the tangled stirrup, tugged, shifted, wrenched, and miraculously felt her foot slip free. Lifting her leg over the horse's back she sat side-saddle for a fleeting second and then she kicked herself off and away from the horse, flew high into the air and went down.

She struck the ground hard, instinctively breaking the fall with her left hand, and lay there stunned, feeling the blessedness of the earth beneath her. After a moment she lifted her head, found her neck intact, rolled over on the ground and stared at her left hand lying inert on the pebbles beside her. *Odd*, she thought, wondering vaguely why she could neither lift it nor feel it as an appendage.

She was still staring at it when Peter rode up to her, flung himself from his horse and ran to her side.

"My God, are you hurt?" he cried. "Believe me, it wasn't supposed to be like this."

Wasn't supposed to be like this . . . what an extordinary thing for him to say, she thought.

"Mrs. Pollifax, are you *all right*?"

"It's my left hand," she told him. "It just lies there. Otherwise," she added with a return of spirit, "I'm basically fine. Perhaps a little in shock, perhaps a little dazed. Yes, definitely a little dazed." She placed her right hand underneath her left one and lifted it. Cradling it and supporting it, she sat up. "But what," she demanded, "happened to that damn runaway horse?"

Peter said, "Can you stand up?"

"Of course I can stand up, just give me a minute."

"But I *can't* give you a minute," he cried despairingly. "I can't, damn it—this is where I disappear, don't you see? Oh damn it, Mrs. Pollifax—Emily—I'm sorry, believe me I'm sorry. I stuck a burr under that horse's saddle so that he'd run away with you, poor devil. Except I was so sure I'd catch him long before the top of the mountain. I thought—oh hell, we don't have *time*. I never expected this, can you ever forgive me? Is your wrist broken?"

"Probably," she said calmly. "Where are the others?"

"I told them I could handle it—bring you back okay—but heaven only knows how much time we have before they—"

"Yes," she said, and told herself that she could put all this together and recover later; she could even understand the sense of what he'd done. "Help me up," she said, giving him her good hand. "I thought it was going to be the waterfall. What happened to that horse?"

He groaned as he helped her to her feet. "I feel like a murderer, he crashed down into the river. It's got horrible currents, it's the same one I had to cross to reach X's camp. I haven't looked but I saw the horse go down. *Heard* him, too, it was ghastly.''

She nodded. "And now you disappear too?"

"Yes, supposedly drowned in this river and swept away while trying to rescue you but of course I was really going to backtrack into the mountain to the cave.''

She nodded. "Then it's a very good thing the horse met with such an accident, I really have nothing personal against him but it will fill out the picture. Yes, definitely it supports your being drowned and swept away.''

Peter looked at her in astonishment. "You're right, I hadn't thought of that; am I in shock too, I wonder? But I can't leave you like this. Does your hand hurt? It's swelling already.''

Standing, she gave a shaky laugh. "Of course you can leave me like this. Yes my wrist hurts, but mostly it feels numb, as if a spring has broken inside—a very interesting feeling, actually, but never mind that. For heaven's sake, Peter, where's your professionalism? *Go!*''

Behind them a pleasant and very familiar voice said, "Nobody's going anywhere, at least not without me.''

They wheeled to see Joe Forbes standing several paces behind them, still smiling, still looking affable except that in his hand he held a small snub-nosed efficient pistol. Far behind him at the foot of the hillside she saw a horse tethered to a tree and guessed it was his. Neither had heard him approach over the pebbles and gravel of the desert floor.

"*So you're the one,*" she said, nodding.

"The one what?" demanded Peter. "What the hell's the matter with you, Forbes, pointing a gun at us, have you lost your mind?''

"Don't,'' Mrs. Pollifax told him. "We've been working for the Russians without knowing it, Peter. I've suspected this ever since Sheng told us we were followed into the desert. It's been a trap, Peter.''

"Trap!'' he cried. "You mean Carstairs—''

"Carstairs doesn't know. The Russians simply leaked the information and sat back to watch us do all the dirty work, and now I believe you're meeting your first KGB man, Peter. Take a long look.''

Peter stared at Forbes in horror. "KGB! *You*?''

"Held in abeyance,'' said Mrs. Pollifax. "A 'sleeper,' I believe they're called. Wonderful credentials, very American, too. Waiting for you to locate and free Wang, after which he was supposed to snatch the prize from you at the last minute and run with it to Moscow. The Russians never planned any attempt to free Wang, we were to do the job for them.''

Forbes said dryly, "Only one thing wrong with that, Mrs. Pollifax—not Forbes *was* to snatch—*is* to snatch the prize. Right now.'' He made circular motions with his gun, directing her to move to one side. "It's Peter I have business with—get away from him.''

"No,'' said Mrs. Pollifax, feeling all her senses giddily heightened by pain. "No I'm not going to move. Not one inch, thank you. You can't possible expect Peter to tell you where Wang is.''

Forbes smiled a lethal smile. "No, but he's going to *show* me where he is. I speak Chinese better than I let on, and I know the Sepos are searching these mountains for a prisoner who's missing from a labor reform camp somewhere nearby. Somehow you got him out and hid him, and I want him.'' He waved his gun menacingly again. "We're running out of time and—''

"Yes that *is* a problem for you,'' said Mrs. Pollifax cheerfully. "The lack of time. How are you going to handle *that*?''

He gave her a pleasant glance that held touches of a

sneer in it. "Shut up," he said, and turned to address
Peter. "Either both of you go with me now, taking me to
Wang Shen—both of you—or I'll kill your friend Mrs.
Pollifax here and now. In front of you, so that you can
watch her die."

It was important that Peter not believe this. "How
absurd," she told Forbes hotly. "You'd kill us both after we
take you to Wang anyway, I'm sure that Peter can't possibly fall for *that*." She gasped. "Oh damn—Peter—sorry—I
think I'm going to faint." She stumbled backward toward
a small mound of stones and sat down, putting her head
between her knees.

Peter started to move toward her but Forbes stopped
him. "You've already lost *her*," he said contemptuously.
"What a ridiculous accomplice they gave you, an old
woman who faints at the drop of a hat. A boy and an old
woman . . . typical American ineptness."

"To hell with you and your assumptions," Peter said
angrily "She broke her wrist, damn you, and—"

From her seat on the rocks Mrs. Pollifax cautiously
lifted her head. She had only pretended to feel faint;
actually she had never felt so keyed-up, or so alive, but it
had seemed a convenient way to put distance between the
three of them and now she saw that Peter and Forbes were
confronting each other so intensely that she was forgotten.
Her good right hand found and curled around a smooth
stone under her foot. As Forbes opened his mouth to retort
to Peter she lifted her arm and hurled the stone at Forbes.

It hit him on the shoulder, doing him no harm, but it
threw him off balance. He fell back and before a startled
Peter could move—before Forbes could even regain his
balance—Mrs. Pollifax was on her feet and in motion,
dealing Forbes a quick karate shin-strike and then a slash
to his temple. Forbes collapsed to the earth without a
sound, his arms outstretched, his eyes open and vacant.

"My God," gasped Peter, rushing to him and prising the gun from his slackened fingers. "My God, Mrs. Pollifax, only brown belt you said?"

"Yes," she said, kneeling beside Forbes, and abruptly she stiffened. "What's worse—oh dear—I believe he's dead, Peter."

"Worse?"

She said unsteadily, "I've only once killed a man—in self-defense, in a cornfield in Albania. I hoped—*so* hoped—" Her voice trembled; she pulled herself together and looked around them. "You'll have to do the rest, Peter, I can't."

"Can't what? Do what?"

Think, she told herself, *think*, be strong for a little longer. She said in a steady voice, "He made one mistake, Peter, he should have simply followed you when you disappeared, without declaring himself, and killed you when you led him to Wang. And now he's dead and you're not, thank heaven, but we have to think and act quickly." She stood up, drawing new strength from being erect. "We have to change how things look—everything," she told him. "They have to find Forbes' body here, you see that, don't you? The two of you disappearing is too much. There has to have been a fight between you both. A fight *here*." She nodded. "It may even be better this way, Peter, but *you've* got to do it."

"Do what?" he asked blankly. "Am I in shock? I can't think!"

She nodded. "My horse ran away with me—they all saw that. The horse is dead in the canyon. I have a broken wrist. You rescued me. Forbes followed and there was a fight and he killed you."

"But a fight about *what?*" he cried.

"Something—anything," she said impatiently, "it doesn't matter. What you have to do now is this." She pulled the long souvenir knife she'd bought in Urumchi out of her pocket and drew it from its sheath. "We need blood, Peter—lots of blood. Carry him to the edge of the water, and I think—yes, quickly, I'll smooth away the tracks from your dragging him . . . He should have your Mao jacket clutched in one hand, or the bloodied sleeve of your jacket. *Something* of yours. And his face should dangle down, as if he struggled to reach you as you went over the side into the rapids. But there has to be blood."

"God," said Peter so devoutly that she felt it was said in religious awe.

Peter removed his Mao jacket.

"Tear it a little," she told him as he dragged Forbes' body toward the gap in the earth. "And—I'm sorry—but please knife him in the heart now, while he'll still bleed. There *has* to be blood," she repeated passionately, stubbornly.

He gave her one quick incredulous glance as he grasped the knife and leaned over the body. "Better not watch," he said, and she was glad to turn away.

When she looked again there was a great deal of blood both on the ground and on the jacket. "Knifed him in the aorta, I think," Peter said curtly, pressed the sleeve of the bloodied jacket into Forbes' hand and then shrugged himself into the remainder of his jacket.

"Toss the knife into the river," she told him. "It has your fingerprints on it."

"What else?" asked Peter, deferring to her.

Mrs. Pollifax looked around, her adrenalin glands racing, her mind operating with a cunning she'd forgotten that she possessed. Forbes lay at the edge of the canyon, his head and one arm dangling over its side, the bloodied rag of a jacket clutched in the hand that lay at his side. Below him—quite horribly—lay the horse, sprawled across a rock just above the racing stream, and quite dead. "Fingerprints where they should be," she said with a nod, ticking off the details. "Your jacket but his blood. I think the picture's complete—now *go*, Peter—go fast."

Peter stared at her. "But—what will you tell them? Mrs. Pollifax, what will you tell them? Why did Forbes and I kill each other?"

"I'll say . . . I don't know what I'll say," she told him. "Leave it to me, Peter—just go. Hurry. Your job's only just beginning."

"But so is yours," he pointed out. "And you're stuck with—"

She said fiercely, "Peter, you're an agent, sufficiently christened and bloodied now, with Wang and Sheng out there waiting for you. Don't bleed for *me*, you've got work to do."

"Yes," he said, staring at her, "except—oh damn it, I want to say—to tell you—" He reached out his hand and gently touched her broken one.

"But you don't have to say or tell me anything," she told him, the tears rising to her eyes, and with her good hand she met his extended fingers and grasped them. She said shakily, "Oh Peter, I'm always saying good-bye to brave and courageous people."

The tension in his face dissipated as he smiled his very rare warm smile. "And I'm saying good-bye right now to a very brave courageous person. Except it can't be good-bye . . . If I ever get out of this—" He leaned over and kissed her on the cheek. "Say hello to Cyrus for me, and marry him, will you?"

He turned, gave a glance at the carnage around them, shook his head over it and began to run, toward the north and toward the deep forest.

'Say hello to the Queen of Sheba for me," she called after him, and then, in a whisper, "God bless you, Peter." She stood watching him until he disappeared among the

trees, and only then did she begin walking tiredly toward
the mountain down which she and the horse had catapulted.
She had just reached the first line of trees and had begun to
ascend when she was met by men with horses, Kazakhs
who had come to look for her.

▯▯▯▯▯▯▯▯▯▯▯▯▯▯▯▯▯ 14

THE CORRIDORS WERE BROAD AND DUSTY—THERE SEEMED
to be dust everywhere in China, she thought blurredly—
but in the halls of a hospital it was unexpected. Everything
she saw held a surreal quality, filled with intimations of
violence: a young woman rushing up a staircase, her white
jacket stained with blood; a young worker wiping up a
pool of blood in a corner, a patient with a bloody bandage
around his head being supported by two orderlies, Army
guards stationed at the end of each hall, leaning casually
against the walls, their faces blank.

She refused anesthesia. The doctor was a young woman,
her soft dark hair plaited into braids, face serious, her
white jacket worn over cotton pants. Consultations were
held with others—she was still a tourist, Mrs. Pollifax

noticed, wondering for how long she would be treated as
one. A young man with a wide eager smile tried a little
English with her. Again she refused anesthesia and a
hospital bed for the night and hoped that no one would
guess it was because she feared what she might say under
anesthesia. She was given a local injection and her hand
strung up on a traction bar while the young woman
manipulated, kneaded, tugged, and pressed the bone into
place.

"A *bad* break," the young man translated for her, and
when the doctor had completed her manipulations she
began winding gauze around her arm, finishing it off with
wet plaster. She found herself encased to the elbow.

"No acupuncture?" she quipped, feeling that the numbing weight of her broken hand now dominated her entire
body like an aching tooth that turned even her thoughts
jaded.

"Pliss," he said, smiling his toothsome smile. "We
treat you American way, all of us being most sorry you
have had this accident in our country."

Mrs. Pollifax gravely accepted this apology and thanked
them all. In the hall outside she found Malcolm and Mr. Li
waiting for her, and at sight of Malcolm she promptly
burst into tears. He handed her a handkerchief and hugged
her. "You're still in shock," he told her. "Hang in!"

In shock yes, but not entirely from the wrist, she
remembered, and knew that she didn't want to think yet
about that horrible scene at the river, and of Peter leaving.

Malcolm said, "I wanted to come with Mr. Li and tell
you."

"Tell me?" she repeated, and glancing at Mr. Li she
saw that his poise was shattered, he looked distraught and
anxious.

"Yes," Malcolm said. "It's your turn to be interviewed
by the police and the fact that you're in pain and shock

doesn't seem to move them at all. They insist on seeing you now."

"Yes," she said, quite understanding why. "You don't look terribly well yourself, Malcolm."

He smiled wryly. "We've all had a shock, of course, but I begin to suspect that Jenny's raisins are doing us all in." He made a face. "George is sick back at the hotel and Jenny's back in bed, and bed is where I'm heading next."

"And Peter and Forbes are dead," she added, wanting to make it real to her, wanting to fix it firmly in her mind that Peter too was dead, not just missing, not gone to meet X and Sheng, but dead. "Have they found Peter's body yet?" she asked.

"I don't think so," Malcolm said. "We've all given statements but we've not been told anything." Mr. Li made a sound in his throat and Malcolm added, "Oh yes, and we're not supposed to talk about it. I promised, we all did, because you're the only one who can tell the police what happened, you see."

She wondered what time it was and how many hours had passed since she had stumbled toward the woods and had been met by the Kazakh horsemen. She dimly recalled being lifted up behind one of them and carried back to the long meadow where she had been delivered to Mr. Li and placed at once in the bus. There had been what seemed an interminable wait after that, until finally Mr. Li arrived with the others and told them stiffly that they must return to Urumchi now, there had been a bad accident and both Mr. Fox and Mr. Forbes were dead. She remembered that Jenny had screamed and then gone into hysterics until Malcolm slapped her face. She remembered Iris examining her wrist and giving her two aspirin and a bottle of warm beer with which to wash them down, and then Mr. Li had insisted that no one talk. After leaving the others at the hotel she had been driven to the hospital in a gray car with curtains at the windows—another shanghai car—and now she was being driven in still another gray car to the security police.

Not the same car, she decided, for there had been a cigarette hole burned in the upholstery of the other one; either the hole had been mended during her hour at the hospital or it was a different car, and she wondered why it mattered, but the smallest things seemed to be of vast importance just now, they kept her from being afraid.

My zero hour, she thought numbly. Peter had experienced his and acquitted himself, and this was hers, and this was why Bishop had been afraid for her, except that no one had known that she would have a broken wrist and feel so oddly dazed for this interrogation.

She was ushered into still another spartan room: a table, several folding chairs, and bare walls except for the ubiquitous photographs of Lenin, Chou, and Mao. It was very similar to all the other rooms they'd been ushered into, but there would be no tea-and-briefings here. The man sitting at the table looked incredibly young; an older man stood looking out of the window, his back to her; he wore a charcoal gray Mao uniform, while the young man facing her was in khaki, with two pockets in his tunic. She remembered that Peter had told her pockets were the only sign of rank in the PLA . . . *which Peter had told her . . .* The thought of Peter brought tears back to her eyes; she allowed them to remain, not hiding them, recalling— ironically—that they were appropriate for this occasion, if for the wrong reason.

She glanced at Mr. Li, who had taken the chair farthest away from her, as if to disassociate himself completely. He looked pale and rather miserable and she realized they must have been giving him a hard time. She thought drearily, *I'm going to have to fight for his future, too.*

Her interrogator was keeping her waiting as he shifted a number of papers in front of him. Where Mr. Li's face was round, this young officer's face was long and narrow. The horror of it, she realized, was that Peter and X and Sheng might already have been found, either in their cave or near it, and these two men know this. Certainly they must already have begun the search for Peter's body . . . Was the water deep enough to hold a body captive? If Peter had miscalculated, would the very absence of a body lift their suspicions about his death? At what point, she wondered, might they begin to search the mountain slopes instead?

If they knew too much, then every word that she spoke would be a recognizable lie, and they did not like spies here. Chinese jails . . . oh, Cyrus, she thought bleakly, and wished with all her heart that she wasn't so *tired*, wished that a broken wrist would radiate violent pain instead of this strange numbing ache that was exhausting her by its subtlety and consistency. It was hot in this closed-up dusty room, too, and the shock—"I've got to stop thinking like this," she told herself sternly. "Think of Cyrus . . . dear Cyrus . . . or Bishop. Or Carstairs. Or geraniums." Anything except what had happened back there by the stream, and of what could have gone wrong.

She wished the man by the window would turn around, but he remained obdurately at the window, his back to her.

The young officer put aside his sheaf of papers and looked at her. He said without expression. "I am most sorry that such a tragedy has occurred. I must ask you questions and discover how such a thing happened and who is to blame."

She said politely, "It has been—for all of us—a tragic loss, a terrible one, and I don't see how anyone can be blamed."

The officer said curtly, "Mr Li—"

"Oh, certainly not Mr. Li," she said firmly. "Mr. Li has shown nothing but courtesy and kindness to us all. A very excellent guide."

Mr. Li gave her a startled glance and then returned his gaze to the floor; perhaps he had not expected equanimity.

"But Mr. Li and this riding of horses—"

She shook her head. "You don't understand how it was," she told him earnestly. "We all watched the Kazakhs perform, and they were magnificent," she emphasized, "but everyone except myself had ridden before, and could ride very well. And Americans"—she hesitated and then looked him straight in the eye—"Americans do tend to be assertive about things they want to do. Peter was the first to ask for a horse to try, and the Kazakhs were *most* polite and let him climb on one, and they obligingly led him up and down the meadow on a rope until they saw that Peter knew horses and really could ride." She stopped, aware that she was flooding him with trivia. "Anyway, they very courteously allowed him to gallop up and down by himself, and then the others pleaded for the same chance but Peter insisted I be put on a horse next. Because I'd never ridden one. Because he thought I should have a picture taken of myself on a horse."

With exquisite irony the officer said, "And did he take your picture?"

"I don't know, the horse ran away with me. And the Kazakhs were certainly not to blame," she put in quickly. "We were all laughing together, and they understood our having fun and were very obliging."

"And Mr. Li?"

"Standing and watching," said Mrs. Pollifax. "Helping to translate the interest in the horses and smiling at our pleasure." He hadn't been smiling, he'd been glowering, but never mind that, she thought.

"And so the horse ran away with you," pointed out the officer, glancing down at his notes.

"Yes."

"And Mr. Peter Fox followed you on horseback."

"Yes."

He waited and then said smoothly, "Yes. Now we come to the important part, please. Your horse 'ran away' as you say, and once over the mountain you came down to the flatland with Mr. Peter Fox in pursuit."

His English was excellent; she wondered if he'd ever lived in the United States but dared not ask. "The horse galloped, or whatever they do," she pointed out, "and my right foot was caught in the stirrup and when I saw the river ahead I knew I had to—absolutely *had* to—jump off."

He was watching her very closely now. "Yes. You succeeded in freeing your foot?"

She nodded. "Yes, I'd been trying to for some time but—I guess desperation helped. And I jumped off and broke my wrist."

The man standing at the window abruptly turned to look at her for the first time, and her glance swerved to meet his. At once she was sorry that she'd looked at him because his gaze unnerved her. The younger officer had been observing her with a professional efficiency, but the eyes of this man were penetrating and alert. She thought, *He is very much the younger man's superior and he's been listening to me, measuring each inflection and nuance, and now he is going to watch my face, my eyes, my hands.* Yet he did not look unkind; his iron-gray hair matched his charcoal Mao suit, and his face was that of a scholar.

She turned her attention back to the young man at the table. "I see," he was saying politely, with a glance at the cast running up her arm. "And where was Mr. Joseph Forbes?"

She shook her head. "Nowhere to be seen. It was Peter—Peter Fox—who galloped up and slid from his horse and ran over to me. I discovered my wrist was hurt and he helped me up and we were standing there talking about what to do . . . Actually Peter was apologizing."

"Apologizing?" he repeated.

"Yes, for insisting I mount the horse. And then very suddenly Joe Forbes was there, he'd left his horse in the woods and walked, and this startled us."

"And then?"

She kept her eyes resolutely on the young man behind the table. "He became very abusive to Peter. He called him names for allowing me to get on the horse, and he said—he also called him names for taking advantage, as he called it, of Iris Damson." She had thought about this and now she delivered it. "He called Peter an out-and-out— should I mention the word?"

"Please," he said.

"Bastard," said Mrs. Pollifax. "And that's when Peter hit him in the stomach and I fainted."

"You fainted," said the young officer, and gave her a thoughtful glance.

"I fainted," she told him firmly.

"I see. So you will presently," he said smoothly, "tell me that you do not know what happened during the next few minutes."

She met this with a lift of her chin and an edge to her voice. "I would like to point out that I had experienced a runaway horse, believed that my life was about to end, I'd thrown myself off and broken a bone, and although I daresay it affords you some amusement to hear that I fainted, faint I did."

"Yes," he said, with an appreciative smile. "And when you came out of this faint what did you see?"

"Exactly what I assume you saw if you have visited the

area,'' she told him. ''Peter was nowhere to be seen, and there was all this blood, and Joe Forbes was lying by the river. I limped over to him and saw that he was—quite dead.'' She shivered. ''After a while I realized it was part of a Mao jacket Mr. Forbes was clutching in one hand, and Peter—Peter had been wearing one. That's when I had the horrible realization that Peter might be dead, too. Have you found him?''

''No,'' he said shortly.

She decided that she believed him. ''What,'' she asked him, ''do you want to find out? It's such a terrible thing, we're all very upset, and I don't understand—''

He said, ''We have never had such an event occur. Naturally a tourist becomes ill now and then, but this is a murder.''

''Yes,'' said Mrs. Pollifax, and was acutely aware of the man standing by the window watching her; she willed herself not to look at him.

The young officer shuffled his papers. ''Mr. Li has told us there was something between this young Peter Fox and Mrs. Damson that might have provoked the quarrel. Mr. Li said he found Peter Fox missing an entire night in Turfan, and the next morning Mrs. Damson explained that Mr. Fox had spent the night with her. This is true?''

Mrs. Pollifax winced. ''I heard her *say* that, yes.''

''Why do you wince?''

''I hoped it wouldn't come to this. I really know nothing about it. I just heard her say it.''

''But you did hear it said. Did they spend much time together, these two people?''

Mrs. Pollifax shrugged. ''No more than with any of us. We were usually all of us together.''

''In this country such matters are frowned on. In your country it is different?''

She sighed wearily. Obviously it was different here—all

those unisex Mao jackets, for one thing—but she felt too jaded to explain her own country, to point out the variables, the multitude of codes, the generation gaps, the sexual revolution, the mores and traditions of courtship. She said, "Not necessarily. Why don't you ask Iris—Mrs. Damson?"

He said coolly. "Already we have, I assure you."

"Good," she said in relief.

"She continues to weep," he added with irony, "and to say as little as you do, Mrs. Pollifax."

She said dryly, "I *feel* as if I've been talking forever."

He drew out a sheet of paper and read from it. "I quote Mrs. Damson. 'Yes Peter spent the night in my room. I don't suppose you'll believe me when I say it was perfectly innocent. He came in to talk, about nine o'clock I think it was. He said everyone else had gone to bed and did I have any books he could read. I didn't. He stayed, talking—on the other bed, curled up—and then he suddenly fell asleep. So I just brushed my teeth—I was already in pajamas—and left him in the one bed while I went to sleep in the other.' "

Dear Iris, thought Mrs. Pollifax, *magnificent Iris*. To the officer she said, "I can believe that, you know. Iris is a very casual person."

He said irritably, "But if this Peter was not in love with her why should he argue, fight, and kill Mr. Forbes over her?"

"Perhaps," said Mrs. Pollifax cautiously, "he felt a very warm friendship toward Iris, and Mr. Forbes said something insulting about her. But really I don't know, it has all been—simply awful. I wonder," she said truthfully enough, "if the explanation will ever be found."

He said sharply, "It is very surprising to me that none of you has any explanation at *all*. A man is dead, Mrs. Pollifax, and another presumed dead for the moment. None of you appears to have noticed anything between Mrs.

Damson and this Peter, or between Mrs. Damson and Mr.
Forbes. Only Mr. Westrum—"

Mrs. Pollifax looked up.

"Ah—a reaction, I see."

"Yes," she said, nodding. "I think George Westrum is
or was in love with Iris Damson."

"Quite a *femme fatale*," said the officer with a touch of
sarcasm.

Mrs. Pollifax smiled faintly. "Yes. But if there was any
triangle, as we call it in America, it seems far more
realistic that George Westrum would have been furious at
Peter." She leaned forward and said with urgent sincerity,
"Look, Mr.—Mr.—"

"Mr. Pi."

"Thank you," she said, and turned her gaze squarely on
the man by the window. "And yours?" she asked coolly.

He bowed slightly, looking amused. "I am Mr. Chang."

"I want to point out to you both that we're all terribly
tired, and I'm sure that none of us cares to go on with the
tour now. When can we leave? As group leader I have to
emphasize that several of us are ill, and all of us deeply
upset . . ." *If anything happens get that tour group the
hell out of the country*, she remembered, and looked chal-
lengingly at Mr. Pi.

He said quietly, "You will all remain here, of course,
until Mr. Peter Fox's body is found."

She struggled not to show her dismay. "That will be
soon, I hope?"

He said without expression. "But of course. You may
go for now, Mrs. Pollifax, but naturally this will continue
tomorrow."

"Naturally," she said, and as she arose she really did
feel like fainting, caught her breath, steadied herself, and
then thought, *"Oh why bother?"* and sank to the floor,
welcoming the oblivion.

*   *   *

It was nearly dark when Mrs. Pollifax was driven back to the hotel in the curtained gray limousine with a silent Mr. Li beside her. Reaction was rapidly overtaking her: since last entering the hotel she had killed a man, seen Peter vanish into the hinterlands of China and into heaven only knew what perils; she'd suffered a runaway horse, a broken wrist, a hospital, and her first police interrogation in China. She supposed that it was not particularly odd of her to want to find a dark corner and cry. Actually, she decided, to cry was not enough: she would prefer a scream.

She would not, of course, be allowed a scream.

She said good night to Mr. Li and walked alone into the empty lobby, turned down the long hall past the souvenir counter, and entered her room. She turned on the lights and stood there, waiting for tears, even a sob, and when none came she sat down on her bed and stared blankly at her white plaster arm and thought of Peter. Hearing a soft knock on her door she lifted her head, considered not answering and then called out, "Just a moment," and then, "Come in."

It was Iris, awkwardly tiptoeing and carrying a tray. "I heard you come in," she said. "I'm next door to you again. I brought you a pill."

Mrs. Pollifax shook her head. "I don't need a pill."

"Ah, but it's a codeine pill," Iris told her. "I've got this doctor back home who gave me supplies for every possible emergency, bless him. Very sensible man, insisted I bring a few pain-killers along in case I broke a leg miles from nowhere. You'll need it before long, you know, it'll hurt tonight."

"It hurts now," admitted Mrs. Pollifax. "How are the others taking this?"

"Oh forget the others," Iris said cheerfully. "It's you I've been worried about ever since the Kazakhs brought you back, you look as if you're going to freak out if you're not careful. I've got some brandy, too, and I think after the brandy you should wash down the codeine tablet with a cup of tea. Doctor Damson, that's me. I don't know how long you've been doing this sort of thing—''

Mrs. Pollifax stiffened. "What sort of thing?"

Iris handed her a glass. "Hold this while I get the tea steeping," she said, and became very busy. She poured hot water into cups from the sterilized-water thermos, ran her hands under the table, disappeared into the bathroom for a few minutes and returned with a second glass, became interested in examining the curtains before she pulled them closed, turned on the table lamp, peered inside and behind it, then glanced under both chair and bed, and finally poured them both brandy. "I don't think it'll hurt me to have some of this too," she announced. "Everybody's sick—*everyone*—Jenny with hysterics, Malcolm's just come down with the same cramps Jenny had yesterday, and George with some kind of dysentery."

She sat down on the edge of Mrs. Pollifax's bed and gave her a radiant smile. "Let's make it a toast, shall we?" and clicking her glass against Mrs. Pollifax's she said lightly, "Shall we drink to Peter?"

Mrs. Pollifax stared at her. "To—Peter?" she said, wetting her lips.

"To Peter," Iris said, and tipped her glass back and emptied it. Leaning over Mrs. Pollifax she pulled back the blankets, pounded both pillows, got up, and stirred the two cups of tea, tasted one, made a face and picked them up, leaving Mrs. Pollifax somwhat alarmed and very alert now.

"Peter is dead," Mrs. Pollifax told her carefully. "So is Forbes. They hope to find Peter's body tomorrow."

"Oh?" said Iris briskly. "They say the currents in that river are very treacherous, though."

"Yes."

Iris was digging out Mrs. Pollifax's pajamas from her suitcase. She said in the same brisk, conversational voice, "The thing is, you know, I once did some undercover work in Texas . . . I was dancing in this place where they were selling drugs and porno under the table, so to speak, except I didn't know about that until I got approached by the law."

"How very interesting," said Mrs. Pollifax, watching her.

"Isn't it?" Her voice was oddly soothing as it continued without expression, simply stating facts as casually as if she were describing the weather. "I worked for the law for about eight months and I wasn't any heroine, believe me—and by the way, I've just checked your room here for bugs, so nobody else is hearing this—but it was all of it great training for somebody who'd breezed through life never noticing anything. I watched, snooped a bit where I wasn't supposed to, eavesdropped, reported to the undercover guys, and the place got closed up. Besides earning me a citation it left me marked, though. It taught me to notice things. Little things."

"Oh?" said Mrs. Pollifax cautiously.

"Yeah," said Iris cheerfully. "Little things, like a certain young man in our tour group who doesn't speak any Chinese but then one day he stands next to Mr. Li and Mr. Kan while they're telling jokes—or telling *something* funny, obviously—and this young man has to turn his face away to hide his own laugh because obviously he understood every word they were saying."

"How—amazing," said Mrs. Pollifax weakly.

"I certainly thought so. And then his doing so much yawning and napping after we got here to Urumchi, as if he never got any sleep at night . . . not to mention the two of you going over the wall together after we got to Turfan.

I saw that, and saw somebody follow you, too, because you all passed my window, one by one. I was standing there in the dark doing my isometrics, and I think I can guess now who it was who followed you both." She grinned at Mrs. Pollifax. "You're a wonderful actress, no one would ever guess that you're not—but never mind."

Mrs. Pollifax looked at Iris thoughtfully. "You're a remarkable actress yourself, Iris, and now I can thank you for what you did in Turfan. Above all I'm glad to understand why you did it because—"

Iris nodded and handed her the codeine tablet. "I know—it worried you. And believe me, I don't want to know anything more and I'm not fishing, honest." She held up her right hand to emphasize this, as if she were under oath. "Except I've got my own theories and I just want to make sure of one thing: we've been drinking a toast to Peter, right? To maybe long life and double happiness for him?"

Mrs. Pollifax smiled at her warmly. "Iris, I love you," she said, "and I thank you because finally I think I'll be able to cry now. To Peter, *yes*." She emptied her glass of brandy, feeling it reach down to her toes, and then she leaned over and hugged Iris and allowed her to tuck her into bed.

ꛯꛯꛯꛯꛯꛯꛯꛯꛯꛯꛯꛯꛯꛯꛯꛯ 15

THE NEXT MORNING, AFTER A SLEEP FILLED WITH NIGHT-
mares—all of them about Peter—Mrs. Pollifax discovered that she could neither tie her shoes nor comb her hair
with her arm in a cast. Only she, Iris, and the two guides
were well enough to appear at eight o'clock in the dining
room, the others being still sick in their rooms, and after
Mr. Li had tied her shoes for her—surely an act of contri-
tion she thought, looking down at his sleek black head—
and after Iris had brushed her hair for her she was borne
off to visit security headquarters again, this time in the
gray limousine with the cigarette hole in the upholstery.

Mr. Chang was there again with Mr. Pi, and now she
was able to see how immaculately he was dressed, and
how silky the fabric of his charcoal-gray Mao tunic. This

time he sat at the table beside Mr. Pi but his eyes were no less penetrating. There was a tape recorder present for today's interview, and she was asked to repeat her story again from beginning to end. It was surprising how difficult she found this; yesterday she'd been keyed up, still in shock, her efforts focused with such intense concentration that she'd given a superhuman performance, even with Mr. Chang's distracting gaze upon her. Today her hand ached with dreary persistence, she'd not slept well, the plaster cast on her arm felt hot and uncomfortable, and her fingers were swollen. Today she realized, too, how very much Mr. Chang frightened her: she felt that he missed nothing, not even the blink of an eye.

When Mr. Pi had completed his endless questioning Mr. Chang said courteously, in flawless English, "And what were the last words you heard spoken between Mr. Fox and Mr. Forbes before you—er—lost consciousness?"

This was clever—an attempt to catch her out—and she regarded him thoughtfully. "It's hard for me to remember, of course, but—" Reaching for the most outrageous words that might close this line of inquiry she said, "I believe Mr. Forbes was shouting 'bloody bastard' at Peter Fox."

"The quarrel was about Mrs. Iris Damson?"

"Yes," said Mrs. Pollifax calmly. "Also about Peter being young, callow, exploitive, immoral, and taking advantage of a woman traveling alone."

Mr. Chang took this in stride. He said, "You fainted then, but not when you discovered Mr. Forbes dead and Mr. Fox missing?"

She said with equal politeness, "I suppose I fainted at that particular moment from the shock of falling off a horse and breaking my wrist."

"Ah yes, and thus missed everything that happened next," he murmured, and she thought that he looked amused again. "I think you may go now, Mrs. Pollifax,

we shall continue our investigations." He bowed courteously.
"Thank you."

Returned to the hotel Mrs. Pollifax found Iris looking
drawn and tired. "Those damn raisins," Iris cried indignantly. "The ones Jenny bought at the bazaar in Turfan
and so generously shared? I found some and saoked them
for a few hours in my bathroom sink and you wouldn't
believe the hay and dung that floated off them. No wonder
everybody's sick!"

"Mercifully they didn't make you sick," said Mrs.
Pollifax. "Have you had any sleep at all?"

Iris gestured this aside impatiently. "Nothing makes me
sick, I have an iron stomach, and no I haven't slept, but
never mind that. How did it go at security headquarters?"

Mrs. Pollifax said dryly, "Well, I'm still at liberty, as
you can see."

Iris grinned. "Mr. Li told me that Peter and Joe had a
fight over me." Their glances met and there was laughter
in Iris' eyes. "That makes me quite a *femme fatale*,
doesn't it?"

"Exactly what Mr. Pi said," she told her. "Now give
me a report on everyone if you will. After all, I'm group
leader and trying to get us out of here."

Iris nodded. "George is still pretty sick and he glares at
me furiously and won't speak but he let me change his bed
sheets and wash his face with a wet towel."

"Generous of him," said Mrs. Pollifax tartly.

Iris considered a moment and grinned. "Malcolm is
making sketches between trips to the bathroom, but so far
he's kept down two tablespoons of tea so it looks promising.
He also tried to kiss me."

"Shocking," said Mrs. Pollifax, with a smile.

"But it's Jenny who's the problem," Iris said, sobering.
"She's tuned out, I can't get through to her. It's been a

ghastly shock for her, of course, but she's begun to act as if her own life's ended. I wish you'd go and talk to her. As group leader," she added with a faint smile.

Mrs. Pollifax nodded. "I'll go right now. Which room?"

"At the end of the hall, last door. No point in knocking, she doesn't want to see anyone, she'll just say 'go away.' "

"Yes," said Mrs. Pollifax and walked down the hall, opened the door and went in.

Jenny, sitting up in bed, looked at her stony-eyed. "I want to be left alone," she said angrily. "You didn't even knock, you have no right to be here, I want to be left *alone*." Her voice trembled on the verge of hysteria.

Mrs. Pollifax said coldly, "As group leader I have every right to find out how you are, so let's have no more of that nonsense. Is your dysentery better now?" She walked to the window and pulled the curtains open, letting light and air into the room.

"Oh that," said Jenny. "Yes, that's gone."

Mrs. Pollifax moved to Jenny's bed and stood over it, looking down on her. "Then don't you think it's time you left your bed to help? Iris has had absolutely no sleep looking after you all and if you're feeling stronger—"

"Iris again," flung out Jenny. "God if I hear that woman's name once more I'll—I'll—"

"You'll what?" demanded Mrs. Pollifax.

"Kill her," said Jenny furiously.

Mrs. Pollifax shook her head and said gently, "More deaths, Jenny? *More* deaths?"

"She took George away from me, and then she took—took Peter—and—oh damn," she cried out, "everything ends. Everything! I can't bear it."

Mrs. Pollifax sat down on the bed and took Jenny into her arms. "Cry, Jenny, cry hard, get it all out. Try. It will help."

"I don't want to," stormed Jenny.

"Try," repeated Mrs. Pollifax, holding her close.

Jenny gave her one startled desperate glance and began to cry. Her whole body cried until she wrenched herself away from Mrs. Pollifax's embrace and threw herself across the bed to beat her fists soundlessly, furiously against the pillows, her sobs engulfing and shaking her. Presently her sobs grew less passionate, the fist ceased its relentless fury and Jenny glanced at Mrs. Pollifax, gave one last sob and sat up. "Why?" she asked like a child. "Why both of them, and in a fight over *her?*"

Mrs. Pollifax looked at her helplessly; she had been so involved in proving this to Mr. Chang and to Mr. Pi that she'd forgotten it was an assumption with which the others must always live as well. "But you're not crying for Peter or for Joe Forbes, are you?" she asked very gently. "Aren't you crying for Jenny?"

The girl flushed. "I don't see what's wrong with wanting to be happy," she said. "Peter liked me, I know he did. It could have had a happy ending, I know it could have. If he hadn't been killed."

Mrs. Pollifax thought of people passing each other like ships in the night, cherishing illusions, assumptions, and misunderstandings, so rarely *knowing*, and she sighed. She considered leaving Jenny to her illusion but quickly discarded the idea: ruthlessness, she decided, was sometimes the greater kindness: "Do you *really* believe that, Jenny?" she asked.

Jenny sat mutinously, "I don't see why you ask. We were together a lot, you saw that. He liked me."

"Many men will like you," she pointed out.

"They don't seem to have," Jenny told her bitterly. "Everything ends for me. I was engaged to Bill for six months, we traveled together through Europe backpacking, we were going to be married and then he decided he was in love with someone else. And now Peter . . . You must know, being older . . . why doesn't *anything* end happily?''

"Because," said Mrs. Pollifax slowly, "there *are* no happy endings, Jenny, there are only happy people.''

Jenny stared at her in astonishment. "Only happy—but without happy endings how—" She stopped, looking baffled.

"It has to happen inside," Mrs. Pollifax told her. "Inside of *you*, Jenny, not from outside. Not from others but in yourself. You may hate Iris for her persistent cheerfulness, even for her joy in living, but you could learn something from her. You'll find—if you talk to her—that she's had three husbands who seem to have treated her quite abominably, she decided to go to college, against formidable odds, and earned her way as a go-go dancer."

"Iris?" Jenny looked appalled. "But then how can she—I don't get it.''

"No you don't," said Mrs. Pollifax quietly, "and that's your problem. Stop feeling sorry for yourself; relationships aren't business transactions. Get out of bed and *do* something. Some people never grow up but it's worth a try, Jenny, and now if you'll excuse me my wrist hurts and I think I'll prop it up somewhere on a cushion for a while."

Jenny flushed. "Oh, I forgot—your *wrist!* Mrs. Pollifax, what happened, was it broken? Does it hurt a great deal?"

Mrs. Pollifax only gave her a brief smile as she opened the door. "See you later, Jenny," she said, and went out.

Malcolm, when she opened his door, looked up and said cheerfully. "The Sepos seem to have fallen in love with you, it seems forever since I've seen you. How's your broken wing?"

"Tiresome," she said.

He nodded. "Quite a change from that Heavenly Lake

we were supposed to be visiting today. If anyone asks, I'm ready to terminate the whole darn tour and fly home. After all,'' he added with a smile, ''I've progressed to three teaspoons of tea now, I'm practically well.''

George Westrum gave her a hostile glance when she stopped in to see him. ''I'm ready to sue,'' he told her angrily. ''Sue the whole damn tour company for allowing this to happen. I've missed Heavenly Lake today, and tomorrow we're off to Inner Mongolia, and if anyone suggests canceling the rest of this tour they'll have a real fight on their hands. I paid good money to see China, and I'm damn well going to see China!''

''Yes, George,'' said Mrs. Pollifax, and left him to his spleen and went back to endure two more interrogations that afternoon at security headquarters.

⧉⧉⧉⧉⧉⧉⧉⧉⧉⧉⧉⧉⧉⧉⧉⧉⧉⧉ **16**

SHE WAS AWAKENED AT FIVE O'CLOCK THE NEXT MORN-
ing by an anxious-looking Mr. Li. "You are to be taken
to security headquarters now," he told her. "The car is
outside, they want you immediately. At once."

"Before breakfast?" she said in alarm. *"Now?"*

He nodded. "For this I am very sorry," he said, and
from the sympathy in his voice she had a sinking feeling
that the interrogations were to accelerate now and that she
might not be returned this time to the hotel. *They must
have found Peter,* she thought. *There must be something
changed, something terribly wrong.*

"I'll be dressed in two minutes," she told him, and this
time chose a jacket with pockets into which she placed her
last chocolate bar, a handful of peanuts from yesterday's

breakfast, and snapshots of Cyrus and her grandchildren. She walked alone through the silent hall to the lobby, out to the driveway, and climbed into the waiting gray limousine. It was a misty morning, the sun not warm yet; she was again in the car with the cigarette hole in the seat beside her and she tried to remember whether her previous trips in this car had been fortunate or unfortunate. Above all, she wondered if somehow they had discovered that Peter wasn't dead; it had been some forty hours now since she had said good-bye to him.

Once again she was escorted into the same spartan room at headquarters, but this time she was shaken to find only Mr. Chang waiting for her. He sat himself behind the table that had previously been occupied by Mr. Pi. A few papers lay spread out before him but his elbows rested on them and his chin was in his hands; he was staring into space but he glanced up at her arrival and spoke sharply to the guard, dismissing him. He watched her cross the room and sit down on the same plain wooden chair. He said curtly, "Good morning," and shuffled the papers in front of him.

Mrs. Pollifax waited, practicing a calm that she didn't feel.

He said at last, looking at her, "You have maintained— with remarkable consistency—that you were unconscious—in a deep faint—during very important moments, Mrs. Pollifax." He paused, the very slightest hint of a smile passing across his face. "I would like to tell you now, Mrs. Pollifax, that I have been aware since the very first interrogation that you have been lying."

"I'm sorry to hear that," she told him politely, thinking *no holds barred now, off we go.* "I can't think why or how you've reached such a conclusion. Perhaps one might ask why?"

He smiled. "Certain nuances, shall we say? Certain techniques familiar to me?" He stopped, staring at her

with an expression not at all unpleasant, and then he
startled her by leaning forward and saying, "There are no
tapes recording our conversation this morning; there is the
utmost privacy at this hour."

"Oh?" she said, not believing him.

"Yes. You see," he went on, "I consider myself—if I
may be forgiven such immodesty—a long-time student of
character, and in you I have found many of the attributes
of my first wife, long since dead."

She had not expected this diversion. Thoroughly startled
she said, "Oh?"

"At the time of our Revolution," he continued, "she
was a most fervent and conscientious soldier. She under-
went several interrogations—yes, and some torture—by
the Nationalists. Two of the interrogations I witnessed
myself, having been captured with her. She was a small
woman, and very feminine, and she cultivated an innocence that was most deceptive, so deceptive, in fact, that it
saved her life. She was like a rock that could not be
moved." He bowed slightly. "It has been uncanny for me
to see in yourself this same quality, one might say technique?
My wife sustained it even when tortured. I think you
would, too."

Mrs. Pollifax sat very still and held her breath; she had
been right to know this man was dangerous.

"There has been, you see, an autopsy on Mr. Forbes'
body," he told her casually. "He was not killed by the
knife after all, as one might suppose from appearances, but
by a sharp blow of a hand to his temple, a blow so
expertly aimed as to cause instant death." He said musingly,
watching her, "A most vulnerable area . . . I would—
myself—suspect that someone at that scene knew karate."

"I see," said Mrs. Pollifax, feeling a chill run up her
spine.

"Which you, of course, could not have known or seen," he emphasized, "having fainted."

"No," she whispered.

He bowed politely. "Because you and I have been adversaries for these past two days, Mrs. Pollifax, and because you and I are of the same generation. I will tell you quite frankly of a small temptation that I have experienced."

"Yes?" she said, feeling her throat grow increasingly dry.

His smile was ironic. "To move suddenly toward you with a front choke or a middle knuckle punch and see if you would meet my action with a countering karate stance before you had time to think."

Yes, very definitely a dangerous man, she realized, and forced herself to say aloud, lightly, "How very interesting, except what is a counterstance, Mr. Chang?"

He chuckled. "I think you have cultivated an exquisite oriental inscrutability that I should not care to see damaged, Mrs. Pollifax, which is why I brought you here at this particular early hour, for the sake of privacy for us both. You see," he added, "the facts of the autopsy bring a certain insoluble question to mind."

"Oh?" she said.

"One must ask," he said imperturbably, "how Mr. Forbes could have been killed by a strong karate blow when his opponent Peter Fox had already slipped over the edge of the canyon and dropped into the rapids below."

Oh God, thought Mrs. Pollifax, and caught off guard, against her will, she reacted with a start as she realized what had been overlooked during those frenzied moments. Her eyes widened and then dropped. Recovering quickly she forced herself to look at Mr. Chang.

He met her gaze serenely and said nothing.

She said, "Of course it's possible that—" She stopped, realizing that what he said was unanswerable; there had been no thought of autopsies when she'd arranged Forbes's body and there was no longer any possible explanation that could divert this man.

He said gently, sympathetically, "I am not a cat playing with a mouse, Mrs. Pollifax, but I think we understand each other better now."

She could only stare at him. "Maybe," she said cautiously, "but what—how—" She stopped.

"I said that I am not a cat playing with a mouse," he repeated, "which is why I brought you here at this hour, to say to you that you may go now."

Go, she thought wildly, *what does he mean by go.* "Back to the hotel?" she asked, scarcely daring to hope.

He said pleasantly, "Mr. Forbes' body is being flown to Beijing today, to your embassy there, on the late morning plane. You will also be on that plane, land briefly in Beijing, and then be flown at once to Tokyo. All of you."

She gaped at him in astonishment.

"I am in charge of these interrogations," he told her calmly, "and I am taking the responsibility of ending them." He looked at her and said harshly, "I do not know—I find that I do not *want* to know—what took place by the river. Two Americans are dead, and I am satisfied with my verdict of Causes Unknown. I feel—from my aforementioned study of character," he added with a faint smile, "that whatever happened was done out of grave necessity. I therefore have no interest in pursuing this investigation further—or even," he added, "the stomach for it."

She had prepared herself for imprisonment at the very least; she had actually expected worse. She stammered, "I—I scarcely know what to say."

"I'm sure you don't," he said, standing up.

"Except to thank you," she told him, rising with him.

"Thank you for the—the courtesies you've extended me, Mr. Chang. *Shown* me."

He chuckled and with a slight bow said, "You will be taken to the airport, all of you, within the hour. I would like to say in return that it has been a pleasure to know you, however briefly, and it must be hoped," he added with a twinkle, "that we do not meet again. Brown or black?"

She did not pretend to misunderstand him. "Brown."

He nodded. "I myself practice Tai Chi now, but once I too had a brown belt in the martial art of karate." He bowed again, graciously. "Good-bye, Mrs. Pollifax, and I wish you a safe return to your own country.

▤▤▤▤▤▤▤▤▤▤▤EPILOGUE

For her wedding Mrs. Polifax had found a dress that Cyrus pronounced stunning. And so it was, but it was several days before she realized that its colors were a beige and dusty jade-green so that when she looked at it now she saw the cliffs of Jiaohe, the desert of Taklamakan and the clay walls of Xian. And her heart ached for Peter. Not even Cyrus, huge and twinkly and affectionate, could quite dispell her awareness of the weeks passing by and her thoughts of Peter, Sheng, and X struggling to reach safety.

The news that she'd brought Carstairs and Bishop had shaken a number of departments at the CIA. When she had reached Tokyo she had placed phone calls to both Cyrus

and Bishop and then had sat wearily on her bed waiting for
one of them to come through.

It was Cyrus who reached her first. "Emily?" he shouted.
"Damn it, Emily, where are you? My God. Emily, I've
worried—"

"Oh Cyrus, how wonderful to hear your voice," she'd
said, and had burst into tears. "I'm in Tokyo, how was
your trip?"

"My trip be damned, Emily. Are you all right? All in
one piece?"

"Only a broken wrist," she'd told him.

" 'Only!' "

"Cyrus, if you haven't changed your mind about us—"

He'd said gruffly, "Don't be ridiculous, m'dear. Nobody like you. Why?"

"I've missed you tremendously," she'd told him with a
catch in her voice. "Russian roulette can be quite exhilarat-
ing when a person has nothing to lose, but oh Cyrus I
discovered how much I could have lost—so easily—and
almost did."

"When does your plane get in?" he asked, and his
voice was thick with emotion.

"I don't know, I don't know, I've put in a call to
Bishop—"

"I'll fly to San Francisco tonight," he told her, "and
I'll meet every plane from Tokyo until you get there. Don't
leave San Francisco without me," he said flatly, and hung
up.

Almost at once the phone had rung a second time and
the operator was saying, "Your call to Virginia has been
put through . . . Go ahead, please . . ."

Abruptly Bishop came on the line saying, "Mrs. Pollifax,
where are you?"

"Tokyo," she told him. "We're all in Tokyo but,
Bishop—*two* people haven't returned from this tour."

"Two?" he'd said. "I don't understand, did you—"

"Have you a list of the people on the tour, Bishop?"

"Yes, but—"

"Please look, it's important, it's why I'm calling."

"Half a minute," he'd said, and she'd heard the rustling of paper and then Bishop's voice again. "I have the list but what do you mean, *two*? And Peter, what about—"

"You find the name Joseph Forbes there?"

"Let's see . . . yes, Forbes . . . history professor, Chicago."

"The important thing just now is to look into his background, Bishop. How much can I say on the phone?"

"As little as possible."

"There were complications, Bishop, and it very nearly ended badly. The problem has to have begun with the source who gave you the information that took us to China. Do you remember explaining to me how you learned about—er—X? Those boundaries?"

"Good God," he'd said.

"This person on the tour came from the other side of them, if I'm not being too abstract?"

"I'm following you," Bishop told her grimly. "Good Lord, you mean this Forbes—"

"Yes, he's the one."

"Where is he now?"

"Dead," she'd told him, and being nearly exhausted after countless hours without sleep her voice trembled. "It had to be done, Bishop—for the sake of the others. I had no choice."

"Steady there," he'd said softly. "You're telling me that *you* . . . ?"

"Yes."

"I see. All right," he said. "Are you feeling better now?"

"I will soon," she'd told him unsteadily. "I have a

broken wrist but—but the purpose of the trip was salvaged, and somewhere out there, heading for the mountains—I'm sorry, Bishop," she'd said, her voice breaking again, "I'm just so *tired*. And those mountains—"

"It had to be the mountains?"

"He thought so, yes, but the most important message right now is Forbes, Bishop, and whoever—well, betrayed you."

There had been a long pause and then Bishop said, "We've got to get you home as quickly as possible. I'll immediately get in touch with the airlines and demand top priority passage for you. In the meantime, however, we'll start things rolling at once on Forbes, with all the repercussions *that* will bring, for which our eternal thanks, Mrs. Pollifax. Obviously our man in you-know-where is no longer ours."

"No," she said, and then, "Could you, when you learn on what plane I'll be returning, let Cyrus know in Connecticut?"

"Gladly," he said and he, too, rang off.

Several hours later she had been on her way to the airport, and she had been deeply touched by the fact that Iris and Malcolm insisted on accompanying her to the air terminal. They had parted warmly, with promises to write, and before moving through the electronic gate she had turned to watch them go—both so tall and slim, Iris still pushing back her tempestuous hair—and she had seen that they were holding hands.

It had occurred to her at that moment—suddenly and with sadness—that Jenny would now feel that Iris had captured the last man on the tour: first George, then seemingly Peter and seemingly Joe Forbes, and now Malcolm, and she would never know the truth.

As so few of us ever do, she thought, and walked through the gate to fly home to Cyrus.

*   *   *

It was a small and private wedding: Mrs. Pollifax's son, Roger, and her daughter, Jane; Miss Hartshorne; a few members of her Garden Club, and a few members of Cyrus' bird-watching club. Bishop had called to announce that wild horses and assassinations abroad wouldn't keep him away. "Besides," he'd added on the phone, "Carstairs is entrusting me with a wedding gift that he thinks you may like and it's too fragile to mail."

The day was very warm—it was late August, after all—but the chapel was cool. Cyrus, giving her an enormous hug, said, "It's a promise—wander off any time you please, Emily, but damn it, m'dear, never again without me."

"Never," she vowed fervently.

There was a slight delay while the organist searched frantically for a missing sheet of music; they waited patiently in the small room near the rear of the chapel until it became apparent that a mild commotion was taking place outside the door.

Cyrus opened it and Mrs. Pollifax heard Bishop's voice say, "Hello there, from the size of you I think you have to be Cyrus?"

Mrs. Pollifax spun around and cried, "Bishop! Oh do come in!"

He stuck his head inside the door. "It's me, bringing your wedding present. Everybody decent and ready?"

And he walked in, followed by a young man on crutches, wearing jeans, a T-shirt, and a broad grin.

"*Peter!*" cried Mrs. Pollifax.

"Yes," he said, beaming at her.

His face was burned from overexposure, there was a clownlike white paste daubed on his nose, his jaw was peeling, and there was that crutch that he leaned on as he moved toward her. But he was alive. He was well. He'd survived.

"Thank God," she whispered. "Oh Cyrus—Cyrus, this is—"

"No need to say," remarked Cyrus. "It's Peter, of course. Hello young man."

"Told her to marry you," Peter said, with a grin.

Cyrus nodded. "She'll be able to sleep nights now, young man . . . No more nightmares."

So Cyrus had guessed, Cyrus had known. Hugging Peter, her eyes filled with tears, she reached out and groped for Cyrus' hand and then with her other hand she reached for Bishop's too. . . .

About the Author

Dorothy Gilman is the author of several popular novels featuring Mrs. Pollifax. She spends six months each year in Nova Scotia and the other six months in Portland, Maine.

White-haired grandmother...
&
free-lance CIA agent...

DOROTHY GILMAN'S
Mrs. Pollifax Novels